10638726

Match Wits with The Hardy Boys®!

Collect the Original
Hardy Boys Mystery Stories®
by Franklin W. Dixon

Celebrate 60 Years with the World's Greatest Super Sleuths!

THE BOMBAY BOOMERANG

FRANK and Joe Hardy become involved in a case affecting national security when Joe dials a wrong telephone number and gets the Pentagon. Two words—"Bombay Boomerang"—that the boys hear before the line goes dead plunge them into a whirlpool of danger and intrigue.

At the same time, their father is investigating the baffling thefts of mercury shipments occurring along the Atlantic seaboard. The celebrated detective finds himself up against a murderous gang who nearly dispose of him in a cask at the bottom of Baltimore harbor. Frank and Joe's astute sleuthing ability not only saves Mr. Hardy's life, but also links the mercury thefts to the top-secret Super S missile mysteriously stolen from a government arsenal.

In a race against time the three Hardys foil a diabolical scheme to create widespread havoc in the United States. Pulse-pounding excitement fills every page of this suspense thriller.

Joe grabbed hold of a cable

The Hardy Boys Mystery Stories®

THE
BOMBAY
BOOMERANG

BY

FRANKLIN W. DIXON

GROSSET & DUNLAP
Publishers • New York
A member of The Putnam & Grosset Group

PRINTED ON RECYCLED PAPER

Copyright © 1970 by Simon & Schuster, Inc. All rights reserved.
Published by Grosset & Dunlap, Inc., a member of The Putnam & Grosset
Group, New York. Published simultaneously in Canada. Printed in the U.S.A.
THE HARDY BOYS® is a registered trademark of Simon & Schuster, Inc.
Library of Congress Catalog Card Number: 70-100116 ISBN 0-448-08949-1
1993 Printing

CONTENTS

THE
BOMBAY
BOOMERANG

CHAPTER I

A Cry for Help

"THIS gang seems to be operating along the entire Atlantic seaboard," Fenton Hardy said. The world-famous private detective sounded as casual as if he were reporting a routine burglary in Bayport. But his two sons sensed an undercurrent of tension in his voice.

"You're really worried about this one, Dad, aren't you?" asked eighteen-year-old Frank, the dark-haired member of the Hardy clan.

His father nodded. "A little."

"Since it's quicksilver the gang is after," Joe Hardy mused, "they'd naturally operate out of cities like Boston, Baltimore, and Bayport. After all, most of the stuff we import comes from Europe, doesn't it?"

"Right," Mr. Hardy replied.

Joe, who was a year younger than Frank, went on, "I boned up on the subject when we were doing our mercury ionization experiments in high school a few months ago. Spain produces more quicksilver than anyone. And we're among her best customers."

Fenton Hardy stretched his long legs, leaned back in his chair, and looked out the window of his study. "You fellows appear to be way ahead of me," he said with a laugh.

"Just did our homework," Joe quipped.

"But seriously," his father said, "you're both right. Our industries need more quicksilver than we mine in the United States, so we import the stuff to the tune of millions of dollars every year. That kind of money attracts criminals, and the ones involved in the mercury thefts are canny operators, judging by the jobs they've pulled off."

The boys had worked on quite a few cases with their father, a former member of the New York Police Department. Starting with *The Tower Treasure,* they had helped solve many baffling mysteries, their most recent being *The Arctic Patrol Mystery.* The Bayport sleuth was proud of his sons' ability and usually discussed his cases with them.

"As you know," he continued, "quicksilver is one metal that remains liquid at room temperature. Looks something like liquid silver."

"How is it being brought in, Dad?" Joe asked.

"In iron flasks about fourteen inches tall, shaped like milk bottles. Each flask has a strong steel cap that screws down tight to prevent leakage. And a flask is heavy when it's full. Weighs one hundred and thirty-five pounds."

"Which means," Frank put in, "that you can't pick one up and slip it into your hip pocket when nobody's watching. What on earth—!"

His exclamation was caused by the sound of shattering glass as a large object came crashing through the window and landed in the middle of the floor.

Quick as a flash, Joe leaped on it, ready to toss it out the window. The thing might be a bomb!

Suddenly he relaxed with a rueful grin. The object in his hand was a stick about twenty inches long, curved in the middle at a ninety-degree angle.

"A boomerang!" Joe announced. "That means Chet Morton is lurking on the premises!"

"That's our buddy Chet"—Frank chuckled—"introducing himself in his inimitable manner."

"Are boomerangs his latest craze?" Mr. Hardy asked.

"Yes," Frank replied. "Last we heard, he was holed up in his workshop at the farm trying to master the carving technique. Evidently he's started throwing them, and not too accurately, as you can see!"

Heavy feet pounded up the stairs. A plump, freckle-faced youth burst into the study, puffing from his climb.

"Gee, Mr. Hardy, I'm sorry about the window," he apologized with a stricken look on his usually placid countenance. "That was one that got away!"

"The latest one that got away," Fenton Hardy suggested dryly. "Chet, you'll have to be more careful with your Australian artillery. However, there's no harm done as long as the broken glass is cleaned up and the window repaired."

"Right-o," Chet promised, relieved that his errant boomerang had not hit anyone. He headed for the kitchen to get the broom and dustpan.

Chet Morton was the Hardy boys' best friend, and they were resigned to his enthusiasm for one hobby after another, despite the often unexpected consequences. They knew that for all Chet's amiable, easy-going nature, and professed dislike for danger, they could count on him to act with sturdy courage whenever he became involved in one of their adventures.

When Chet left the study, Mr. Hardy told the boys he was leaving for Baltimore to follow a lead in the mercury case. His best bet, he thought, would be to go underground, adopting one of his many disguises, and try to make contact with the thieves.

He would register at a waterfront hotel under the alias of L. Marks. "Here's the telephone number where you can reach me," he said. "Keep it under your hat, or my life may be in danger!"

"What can we do, Dad?" Frank asked eagerly.

"Here's the first thing. On Monday around noon call the number on this slip of paper. It's the Mersex Iberia Company in New York City, area code 212. Get the shipping department and ask if they have anything from Spain arriving within the next ten days."

"Mercury?" Frank asked.

"See if they mention it. But don't let on that that's what you're interested in. If they get nosy, say you're making a survey on Spanish melons. And hang up before they trace the call."

Frank nodded. "Okay."

"We don't want any member of the gang getting wise to the fact that we're on to them," Mr. Hardy went on. "They just might have planted one of their agents in the front office, and also there is the possibility that they're tapping the company's wires."

Later the boys watched as their mother packed the detective's bag. Laura Hardy was a trim, pleasant woman with blue eyes. She worried about her husband's dangerous occupation, but always prepared him with whatever he might need on his assignments.

Mr. Hardy put the records of the mercury case in a large envelope and slipped it into a secret compartment of his suitcase. Joe handed him a coil of fine wire with a small metal sphere attached to one end.

"Don't forget the insect," he said.

His father smiled and took the coil. It was a bugging device that picked up sounds and transmitted them to the receiver at the opposite end.

"I'd never leave without my bug." Fenton Hardy chuckled as he snapped the bag shut. Half an hour later he left for the airport where his pilot, Jack Wayne, was waiting to fly the Hardys' private plane to Baltimore.

The following morning after church services, Frank and Joe drove out to Chet's farm on the outskirts of Bayport. On the way they picked up pretty blond Callie Shaw, Frank's favorite date. The three talked about the next day's cookout at the home of Phil Cohen, a regular member of the group. When Frank briefly mentioned his father's new case, Callie said:

"I hope it won't keep you from the festivities."

"You never can tell when Dad's on an undercover job," Joe responded. "All we know is that he'll follow the trail wherever it leads, and send us an SOS if he needs help in a hurry."

Frank turned the car off the highway, down the dirt road leading to the Morton farm, before giving his opinion. "Looks as if the picnic is safe enough. We don't have anything to do except make a phone call on Monday."

The car jerked to a halt in a cloud of dust as Frank put on the brakes.

"Hi, fellows," Chet called out. He was waiting

for them with a boomerang in his hand. His sister Iola, whom Joe considered his steady date, waved at the trio. "Have a throw!" she invited.

They all began to inspect the boomerangs in the workshop under what Chet termed "my professional direction." He explained that the boomerang is found in many lands, even among the Indians of our Southwest; but the most famous is the Australian boomerang.

"The principle," Chet intoned in a lordly manner, "is that the angle of the arms and the symmetrical planes, plus the torque that moves the ends off the center line, give the weapon an aerodynamic impetus that causes a reverse vector."

"Come again?" Callie giggled, making a face.

Joe winked. They knew Chet liked to talk about his hobbies almost as much as he liked eating.

"In other words," Frank interpreted Chet's explanation, "a boomerang returns to the spot from which it was thrown. And there also are non-return boomerangs, aren't there?"

Chet gave a superior smile. "Of course, but they're the kind you use to bop an enemy or a kangaroo. But I'm more interested in the science of the return boomerang."

Frank and Joe, for all their joshing, were interested in Chet's hobby. Who could tell? A boomerang might come in handy on a case!

"Here, let me have one," Joe said.

They all tried a few throws. But it was not as easy as it seemed, and they began to get a bit discouraged.

Then Joe seized a boomerang in his hand, whooped loudly, and hurled it in a straight line toward the front gate. The weapon whirled through the air at terrific speed, curved to the left, and came back—heading directly for an antique lamp on a post in front of the house!

"Watch out!" yelled Callie.

"Duck!" called Iola.

Chet was terrified. "Do something!" he wailed.

Joe was too far away to do anything. But Frank leaped up and caught the boomerang with one hand just as it was about to crash into the lamp!

"Wow!" Chet said. "That was close. Thanks, Frank!"

"Bad shot," Joe admitted. "Next time I throw a stick like that, it'll be down in the pasture!"

After lunch at the Mortons' Frank and Joe drove home. They were greeted by their Aunt Gertrude.

"Boomerangs!" sniffed the peppery spinster sister of Mr. Hardy when the boys spoke of Chet's latest hobby. "Boomerangs are for the Wild Man of Borneo!"

"Oh, Aunty, they're really a lot of fun," Frank said.

"Fun!" His aunt shook her head. "I would expect you to find a more genteel hobby. Mark my

Frank leaped up and caught the boomerang

words, no good will come of it. Just think of how Mrs. Morton would have felt if you'd broken her antique lamp!"

"Fortunately, we didn't," Joe said contritely. "Anyhow, we'll soon be experts!"

"Humph!" was his aunt's reply.

Frank and Joe drove over to Phil Cohen's on Monday morning to help him with the preparations for the cookout.

Phil was a distinct contrast to Chet. A quiet boy, good with the books, he had an artistic nature. He was slender and agile, quick on the uptake, a useful fellow to have around in time of danger.

The trio went to work at once, setting up the barbecue and hanging party decorations. About noontime, as they finished arranging tables and chairs, Frank asked, "Can I use your phone, Phil? Joe and I promised to make a call for Dad."

"Sure. Business before pleasure," Phil replied with a grin. "Just put your dime in the little box next to it!"

The Hardys went into the house and Joe dialed the number his father had given them. Frank listened in with an ear close to the receiver.

The phone rang on the other end. There was the familiar clicking sound as someone picked it up. "Hello?" said a man's voice.

"Is this Mersex Iberia in New York?" Joe asked.

"No, it's a Washington, D. C. number," the voice answered. "This is area code 202. You want 212."

"Sorry."

"Don't mention it. Happens all the time."

Joe was about to hang up and re-dial when he and Frank heard the party on the other end give a hoarse shout. The words that followed were clearly audible.

"Help! They're after the Super S data! Help! Help!"

CHAPTER II

Mercury Mystery

STARTLED by the shout, Frank and Joe froze. Their experience in crime detection told them to wait for some clue to the mysterious voice, which cut off suddenly.

There was silence for a moment at the other end of the connection.

"Must be a joke of some kind," Joe muttered impatiently. He pulled the phone away from his ear, intending to hang up.

Frank grabbed his wrist with the whispered warning, "Hold on! If thugs have jumped that guy in Washington, we don't want to lose our communications. We might miss the one piece of evidence we need to get on their track!"

Muffled sounds came through the receiver. Drawers banged, locks snapped, and papers rustled as if an office were being ransacked. Men's voices could be heard in hurried conversation.

The boys could not make out what they were saying until the very end when two words came through clearly: *Bombay Boomerang.* Then the line went dead.

Joe turned to Frank with a mystified expression. "Did you hear what I heard?"

Frank nodded emphatically. "Bombay Boomerang. But what on earth does it mean?"

Joe shrugged. "You don't think we may have imagined it?" he inquired doubtfully. "Maybe we've got boomerangs on the brain. If so, we can chalk off one illusion to old Chet and his identified flying objects."

"Well, what about Bombay? I don't recall Chet ever mentioning the Indian city, although he's spouted about ten thousand words concerning Australia."

"It's a puzzle, all right."

Phil came into the house. "Finished?" he asked.

Joe shook his head. "Got the wrong area code."

Phil chuckled. "Try again. Better get it right this time, though, or your father will begin having second thoughts about the reliabilty of his seconds-in-command."

Joe picked up the phone again as Phil walked out to the porch.

"Two—one—two," he counted aloud before dialing the number. A secretary in the Mersex shipping department confirmed without hesitation that cargo was due in from a Spanish port aboard a freighter. Of her own accord she provided the information that it was mercury.

"Okay," Frank said after Joe had hung up. "Now to get through to the Baltimore hotel and let Dad know what we've learned. Perhaps he'll have a theory."

Fenton Hardy was interested to hear about the Mersex cargo. But he became disturbed when Frank related the tale of the wrong-number phone call to Washington.

"This could be of vital importance to our national security," he declared.

"Are you going to call Washington?" Frank asked.

"Yes. An old friend, Admiral Rodgers is one of the top men in missile research, and he's got an office in the Pentagon. I'll talk to him and get back to you later on."

Frank and Joe joined Phil on the porch. "I'm expecting all of you this evening," their friend announced. "My strategy is elementary. The girls can make the hamburgers, the boys will eat them."

"Chet Morton will like that," Joe said, grinning. "Just include a few wedges of chocolate layer cake, some slices of pie, lots of ice cream and soda—"

"Say, I'm getting hungry," Frank interrupted. "We're about due home for lunch. Aunt Gertrude will lecture us if we're late!"

"See you tonight," Phil called as they pulled out of the driveway.

Later that afternoon the Hardys' front doorbell rang. "I'll get it," Frank said to his mother and aunt, who were in the living room sewing.

Two men stood outside. They had a tough look about them, in spite of their fashionably-cut clothes. Frank sized them up. "Plenty of money," he thought to himself, "but a couple of slippery characters all the same."

"Won't you come in?" he said politely. Joe joined the group in the hall.

"We'd like to speak to Fenton Hardy," declared the man in the trench coat and snap-brim hat.

"Yeah, important business," said his partner in the windbreaker and beret.

The boys said their father was away from home. They did not volunteer any information as to his whereabouts.

"Since your father isn't here, maybe you can help us," the first fellow declared in a gravelly voice.

"Not likely!" was the reply that occurred to Joe, but he held his tongue.

"Do you have a Mercury for sale? We were told you advertised a second-hand job. If the price is right, we just might be willing to take it off your hands."

Frank and Joe answered that they had never advertised a second-hand car.

"Oh. Well, maybe we've got the wrong address."

As the two men went out, Snap Brim turned around and mentioned the name of a hotel on the Bayport waterfront. "If you hear of anyone with a Mercury that's in shape for a long drive, let us know! We're in Room 203."

The door shut behind them.

"What do you make of those guys?" Joe asked his brother.

"I don't like their looks," Frank replied. "Where do types like that get enough money to patronize the best clothing stores? If they have money, why are they living in a waterfront hotel? And why would they be interested in a second-hand car?"

"Seems to me we should do a little investigating. Let's go to the hotel and call their bluff!"

Frank went along with that, but another thought occurred to him. "Wait a minute! Biff Hooper's uncle has an old Mercury. Could be he's in the market for a buyer."

Joe put in a phone call and came back with the report. "Affirmative. The old heap is available for the first guy with ready cash who turns up. You know what this does? It gives us a good excuse to visit our new friends—I use that last term loosely."

"New enemies might be more like it," Frank concurred. "Still, we don't have much to go on, except appearances. It could be that the Mercury bit is merely a coincidence."

Joe chuckled. "Will our faces be red if those fellows really want to buy a second-hand car!"

Deciding to take no chances, the Hardys asked their pals Biff Hooper and Tony Prito to accompany them to the waterfront. Both were ready, willing, and able.

Biff, a blond six-footer, knew how to use his fists, and dark-eyed, olive-skinned Tony could always be counted on in a dangerous mission.

The two roared up the driveway a little later in Biff's car. "What's the play?" Tony demanded, jumping out of the bucket seat before the vehicle jolted to a stop.

"How many desperadoes do we corral this time around?" Biff quipped.

"Don't crave too much action," Frank advised. "You might get more than you bargained for!"

Quickly the Hardys filled them in, after which the four headed for the waterfront. Biff parked on a side street near the hotel, a dilapidated building with shingles askew on the roof, and paint peeling off the walls. The neon lights had half the letters missing.

The boys got out and advanced cautiously. The front door was open, revealing the small, dingy lobby. A sleazy clerk sprawled over the desk, reading a newspaper.

After one look, Biff gave his verdict. "My impression is that we're inspecting the place most likely to have a guest list made up of characters from the rogues' gallery."

Tony bobbed his head up and down. "Certainly not the Waldorf-Astoria," he said.

"I know," Frank agreed. "That's why we asked you to come along. There's a slight chance that these fellows are on the up-and-up about the car. But we think there's something phony about them. And we want to know what it is."

"No matter how you slice this salami, we've got to go in there," Joe added.

"Since Joe and I can identify the guys we want to check, we'll go up to their room," Frank continued. "If all we have to do is arrange a deal about a car, we should be back here in two shakes of a lamb's tail."

"If you don't see us pretty quickly, you'll know something's gone wrong," Joe added. "That'll be your clue to come busting in. Let's put a time limit of ten minutes on the operation."

"Roger," said Biff, and the four synchronized their watches. Then the Hardys entered the hotel.

The desk clerk raised his eyes from his paper and gave them a suspicious stare. When they told him the number of the room they wanted, he jerked a thumb toward the stairs and mumbled, "Second floor, third left."

"Pleasant receptionist," Joe observed sarcastically as they climbed the stairs.

They found the room and rapped on the door. It was opened by the man in the beret.

"Well, look who's here!" he said, sounding so threatening that Joe was reminded of the story about the spider and the fly. "Won't you come into my parlor—" he recited under his breath.

Frank and Joe went in. They immediately recognized Snap Brim standing at the window. He came toward them with a menacing scowl. Shaking his fist at them, he spoke with suppressed fury. "So you think we want a car, do you? I'll tell you what we want. Mercury!"

"Your old man is poking his fingers into a hot racket, and we don't like it!" Beret added.

Joe spun on his toes and headed for the door. He was quick, but not quick enough. Beret stepped in front of him. Tall and beefy, he flexed his powerful shoulders, raising his long arms in a wrestler's stance.

"Come on," he barked. "I'm itching to take care of you. Next time you bob up, it'll be in the bay, and you'll be as dead as an iced mackerel!"

CHAPTER III

The Hotel Caper

SUDDENLY the door splintered inward with a terrific crash, dislodging the lock. Biff and Tony hurtled into the room.

"Sorry we haven't been introduced," Tony said to the beefy character, "but I imagine we'll get to know one another real fast!"

"It's all a question of timing," Biff quipped. "To wit, ten minutes!"

Joe covered his relief with a whimsical remark. "We were about to have a ball, just the four of us."

"A brawl!" Frank corrected him.

"A real go-round," Biff added, "only our invitations never arrived. Anyway, the party's over."

The two men were caught off balance. Snap Brim, who had lowered his fist, recovered first. "Okay," he snarled at the Hardys. "So you've got a bodyguard. But next time may be different! And there's sure gonna be a next time! We're not

20

through with you by a long shot, or with your old man, either! You can tell him that!"

Frank, Joe, Biff, and Tony stepped past the door which was crazily swinging on its hinges. The desk clerk, who had heard the noise and came upstairs, looked at them uncomprehendingly as they walked past him and out of the hotel.

"That caper had a happy ending," Tony remarked.

"I wouldn't be too sure it's ended," Frank warned. "The curtain hasn't gone up on act two yet."

A series of rapid-fire explosions dented their eardrums. Down the street chugged an antiquated jalopy—fire-engine red, bucking like a bronco and backfiring explosively with nearly every revolution of the cylinders.

Roly-poly Chet Morton guided his favorite vehicle to a stop at the curb and jumped out. "I've just been to your house," he said. "Your mother says your dad phoned from Baltimore. She looked so worried, I think there's something brewing. You're to contact your father before you do anything else."

The Hardys glanced up at the second floor of the hotel and spotted a scowling face at the window of the room they had just left. Beret stared down on them, a slightly baffled expression on his face.

Had he heard Chet's booming voice clearly

enough to understand the message from Fenton Hardy? If so, it could mean trouble, and plenty of it!

Biff came up with an idea. "Suppose I stay here to keep an eye on these birds? If they come out, I'll tail them. That'll give you a chance to go home and put in that call to Baltimore. We'll meet here later and compare notes."

"I'll keep you company," Tony suggested. "Just in case you need some reinforcement."

"Good thought," Frank said. "Let's go."

"I'll take you in my car," Chet offered.

"And arrive with an aching back!" Joe groaned.

Everybody ragged Chet Morton about his bone-rattling car. But he wheeled it around the busy streets of Bayport, and boasted a good safety record, partly because pedestrians and motorists who heard him coming got out of the way.

Right now the Hardys were glad to have Chet give them a lift to their house. While Chet went into the kitchen looking for one of Aunt Gertrude's specialties which were usually available, Frank dialed the number of his father's hotel. The detective answered almost immediately.

"Let me call you right back," he said. "Stand by!"

A few minutes later the phone rang. Frank picked it up, while Joe ran upstairs to the study to listen in on the extension.

"I didn't want this call to go through the switchboard here," Mr. Hardy explained. "Someone might eavesdrop on us."

"Dad, what's going on?" Frank wanted to know.

"Well, not too much on my end," his father replied. "However, I'm not discouraged. I picked up a few leads that are worth checking out. Right now I'm posing as a hood. It's the best disguise for undercover operations along the waterfront where hoods hang out."

Frank interjected, "Do you realize that the mercury gang is on to you? They came to our house hoping to find you here. And when we went to their hotel to check up on them, they got violent over your part in the case. Said to get off their backs—or else!"

The news surprised Mr. Hardy, who listened grimly to Frank's detailed account of the events that afternoon.

"Obviously word has gotten around that I'm working on the case. You and Joe better watch your step as long as those two mugs are loose in Bayport. It was a good idea to have Biff tail them. Perhaps they'll lead him to something."

"I hope so. What's your next step, Dad?"

"Well, I'm not exactly in the safest spot here. The thieves might even know that Hardy and Marks are the same man."

"If that guy in the hotel heard Chet mention

that you're in Baltimore, they might put two and two together!" Frank said.

"They might and they might not. I have no choice but to continue as L. Marks and play it by ear."

Frank and his father batted the details around to be sure of covering all angles. Finally Mr. Hardy said, "The Bayport pair look like our best bet right now. They probably rank on a lower echelon of the organization and receive strong-arm assignments from the top. They might lead you to the ringleader. Try not to let them shake you and tail them wherever they go."

"Right. I'm sure Biff and Tony will help, too."

"Okay. But at the same time you'd better get the police to back you up. Tell the whole story to Chief Collig. He'll know what to do."

"What about the boomerang bit?" Frank asked, changing the subject.

"That's why I called in the first place. I talked with Admiral Rodgers at the Pentagon. He's very concerned about what you boys heard when Joe made that wrong call to Washington. But he wouldn't give me much information over the phone. Says the matter is top-level security stuff, too hush-hush to discuss outside his office."

"Are you going to see him personally, then?"

"I can't leave Baltimore with the mercury gang on my hands. However, I've made an appointment for you and Joe to meet him. Be at his office tomorrow morning."

"Will do."

"If your friends can't take over the surveillance of the Bayport hoods during that time, Chief Collig will."

"No problem," Frank said.

"So long then. Good luck, and be careful!"

The phone clicked on the other end. Joe came down again and observed that the mystery was thicker than ever. "Which," he continued, "is all the more reason for us to pitch in and give Dad all the help we can."

"Exactly. Let's go to headquarters right away."

They went to the kitchen to tell Chet, who was enjoying a piece of Aunt Gertrude's fresh-baked apple pie.

"Be a sport and drive us over to see Chief Collig," Frank said.

"Whatever you say." Chet stuffed the last bite into his mouth and followed the Hardys outside. A few minutes later they reached their destination.

"Have to double-park," Chet declared. "You two go ahead. I'll wait for you here."

Seconds later Frank and Joe confronted Chief Collig in his office. He was an old-timer who had worked his way up on the force. He understood criminals because he had collared his share, and often assisted the Hardys in their cases.

"Sit down, boys," he said with a smile, "and tell

me what brings you here. A new case, I suppose. That's what comes of having a detective for a father. Maybe you should listen to your Aunt Gertrude more often. She'd find another occupation for you, double-quick!"

The chief stopped kidding, however, when Frank and Joe gave him the facts.

"I'll put two of my men on the case. They can stake out the hotel and check up on those characters."

He made a brief phone call and talked to one of his officers. Then he turned to the boys again.

"Let me have the address and descriptions of the men."

Frank complied.

Collig wrote it down and added, "Tell Biff Hooper to stay there until a green Ford arrives. If he has already left, call me."

"Thanks, Chief."

Chet drove the Hardys back to the hotel. Biff and Tony were still parked in the side street, keeping an eagle eye on the entrance.

"Anything stirring?" Frank queried.

"Not even a mouse," Biff reported. "I've been staring at that door until I'm cross-eyed."

"Our friends are still inside, no doubt," Tony added.

"Let's make sure," Frank suggested.

He and Joe went into the building. Strolling

casually up to the desk, they questioned the clerk about the two suspects.

To their amazement they had checked out. "Paid their bill and left by the back way about an hour ago. They didn't leave a forwarding address," the clerk added with obvious relish at the Hardys' disappointment.

They returned to the car to tell their friends what had happened. Biff and Tony were crestfallen, blaming themselves for flubbing a critical assignment.

"Think we should investigate the desk clerk?" Biff inquired. "He's a slippery fish, a definite suspect as far as I'm concerned."

"Trouble is," Frank replied, "there's no evidence against him. He's about as amiable as a porcupine, but that's no crime. We can always move in on him later."

"Now what?" Joe asked.

"We better call Chief Collig and cancel the backup squad," Frank said. "Or, on second thought, let's wait till they get here and ask them to check out the room. Maybe we'll find a clue."

"Good idea," Joe agreed.

Soon an unmarked police car arrived and two officers jumped out. Frank quickly explained the situation, and asked if he and Joe could join in the search.

"Sure. Come on," one of the men said and went

to the desk. He showed his badge and they were admitted to the room. Their search, however, was unsuccessful. The pair had left nothing!

Dismayed, all four boys returned home. Frank and Joe spent the rest of the afternoon reconstructing the apparently unrelated events that had occurred with such swiftness. There were so many puzzles that didn't make sense—the Bombay Boomerang, the Super S data, the Bayport suspects.

"I don't know where to begin fitting the pieces together!" Joe groaned.

Before his brother could answer, they were startled by a solid object that crashed through a window pane and landed on the carpet amid a shower of glass.

"Chet again?" Frank complained. "Isn't he getting a little out of hand with his boomerangs?"

"Hold it!" Joe interrupted. "That's no boomerang!" He picked up the object, which turned out to be a heavy bolt with a piece of paper wrapped around it, held in place by a rubber band.

Joe spread the paper out on the table. Frank peered over his shoulder. With mounting excitement they read a message written in crude letters approximately an inch high. It was a warning that gave them cold chills.

WE KNOW ALL ABOUT YOU! SPLIT OUT OR YOU'LL WIND UP IN A CEMENT BARREL!

CHAPTER IV

The Battered Car

"WHAT's that?" asked a nervous voice behind the boys. Aunt Gertrude had rushed in to see who had broken the window.

"Just another message," Frank replied, trying to soothe her. "It's hardly worth mentioning."

But her inquisitive eyes had already scanned the words on the paper. "I believe they mean it!" she retorted in frightened tones. "You'd better drop the case right now. I'm not interested in going to a funeral—least of all mine!"

Joe slipped the bolt into his pocket, then phoned Baltimore and asked to speak to L. Marks.

"He checked out," said the hotel clerk. "Packed his bags, paid his bill, and left without giving us any forwarding address. Seemed to be in a hurry."

"Dad must be on to a hot lead," Frank declared. "That would explain why he departed so suddenly. Besides, if he had run into any trouble, he'd have left a code message for us."

Joe nodded thoughtfully. "Let's hope he contacts us before we fly to Washington tomorrow morning."

"Meanwhile, we might as well enjoy ourselves tonight," Frank suggested. "It's almost time to start for Phil's."

The boys went upstairs to tell their mother that they were leaving. Laura Hardy said she was relieved that for once nothing dangerous was involved. Aunt Gertrude sniffed, saying that her nephews were able to find danger wherever they went.

"You look for it hard enough!" she accused them sternly.

Frank and Joe chuckled as they headed for their convertible. Just then a shiny new car pulled into the driveway. It belonged to a friend of Mrs. Hardy.

"Good evening, Mrs. Jackson," Joe greeted the woman at the wheel. "Here, let me help you out."

"Nice little runabout you have there," Frank added admiringly.

"That's a compliment," Mrs. Jackson said with a smile. "I selected it myself. One drive around the block, and I was hooked. It's a gift from my husband for our wedding anniversary, so you can bet I'll take good care of it!"

She went into the house, and Frank and Joe drove to Phil's. Callie and Iola were already there, along with Biff, Tony and Chet, and most of their friends.

"We've got a mystery for you," Joe announced.

"Suppose we get to the chow first," Chet urged, patting his rather expansive waistline. "Mysteries are more solvable when the inner man is satisfied."

Soon the group were enjoying hamburgers and hot dogs, which the girls had barbecued.

"What mystery?" Biff queried.

Joe pulled the bolt from his pocket. Extending it on the palm of his hand, he asked, "What do you make of this object?"

Tony Prito picked it up and examined it. Since his father was a building contractor, he had seen many bolts of all sizes, shapes, and makes. He looked at this one with an expert eye.

"It's a type used in the construction business on the end of reinforced bars," he told the others. "Nothing unusual, as far as I can see."

"What's unusual," Joe observed, "is that somebody pitched it through our window today."

Phil shook his head in mock surprise. "The kind of games you two play!"

Frank nodded. "Great fun. It had a warning attached to it that we might get acquainted with a barrel of cement!"

Their friends immediately became serious. "Maybe it'll tell us something if we can find out where it came from," Chet suggested.

Tony cautioned that the bolt could have come from lots of places. "Every contractor uses this kind of fixture. There must be dozens of warehouses near Bayport where you could find them piled up."

"Isn't that the point?" Biff put in. "The guy who threw Frank and Joe a curve might be in the construction business. If he works for a contractor, he'd have a supply of bolts to pick from whenever he got the urge to go on a window-breaking spree."

"Yes, but if he's a crook, he could have stolen this one," Phil reasoned. "Suppose he slipped into one of the warehouses Tony mentioned and left with the bolt in his pocket?"

Joe turned that suggestion over in his mind. "I don't see the point in stealing a single bolt. Why would anyone go to that trouble when a rock would have carried the message just as well?"

"We don't know that he only stole this bolt," Phil replied. "What if he took a whole shipment? He could have decided to use the bolt as a carrier pigeon on the spur of the moment, because it happened to be the handiest thing available."

Mrs. Cohen came into the room while the discussion was going on. She told Frank and Joe that their mother was on the phone.

Frank took the call. "Hi, Mom," he said.

Laura Hardy sounded frantic. "Come home

right away!" she cried. "Something terrible has happened. Mrs. Jackson is in a state of shock, Aunt Gertrude is having hysterics, and I don't know what to do!"

Frank turned to his brother. "We'd better leave right now."

Calling out a quick explanation to their pals, the boys ran outside and jumped into their convertible.

An appalling sight met their eyes when they turned into the Hardy driveway. Mrs. Jackson's spanking new car, so bright and lustrous when they first saw it, was a total wreck! All the windows were broken. The hood, chassis, and fenders were dented and twisted. The dashboard was smashed in.

Frank whistled. "This car has been wrecked deliberately!"

"And here's the weapon," Joe declared.

He picked up a steel bar from the driveway. About four feet long and a little over an inch thick, it was flecked with paint from the car, and it fitted into the deep dents on the hood. The wielder of the steel bar had pounded the new car into ruins!

But why? Joe pointed to the side of the vehicle. There, written in spray paint, was the warning:

GET OUT OF THE MERC RACKET

"These guys sure want us to get the message," Frank commented. "Nothing subtle. Strong-arm all the way!"

"No wonder the women are in a tizzy," Joe added. "We'd better go inside and see how they are."

When the women calmed down, Mrs. Jackson revealed that she had seen the vandal attacking her car with the steel bar. Her description matched the beefy fellow in the beret!

Frank and Joe exchanged glances, then Frank turned to Mrs. Jackson. "If it's any consolation to you," he said, "this vandalism was not aimed at *you*. Whoever did it made a mistake. He was trying to scare us and thought he was wrecking one of our cars."

"But why anyone would do a thing like that!"

"It has something to do with a new case our father is working on," Joe explained.

Mrs. Jackson shook her head. "It's terrible. Simply terrible."

"Have you called the police?" Frank asked.

"Certainly we have," Aunt Gertrude put in. "They were here before you arrived and surveyed the car. Then Chief Collig called and said you should get in touch with him in case you have any suspicions or clues."

Frank telephoned the chief to confirm that the vandals, no doubt, were the two men they had encountered earlier. He also told Collig about the warning.

"I'll alert all our men in the Bayport area to be on the lookout for those two," Collig said. "Let me know if something new develops."

"Sure thing," Frank promised and hung up. Then he turned to Mrs. Jackson.

"Is vandalism covered by your insurance?" he asked.

"I don't know. Oh, I hope it is!"

"Let me have the number of your agent and I'll find out," Joe suggested.

Mrs. Jackson pulled out a business card from her handbag. "We had the agent over just the other day. Here it is."

Joe phoned the man and learned that luckily the damage was covered. The news helped Mrs. Jackson to regain control over her nerves, and she left shortly afterward in a taxi.

Frank and Joe discussed the latest event.

"Those thugs are determined to get us out of the way," Joe declared, "and they have no scruples about how they do it!"

"When they realize that we won't give up, they'll undoubtedly use even more drastic methods," Frank added.

Aunt Gertrude had another fit of hysterics. "Attacked by brutes who think the Hardy family's concerned about their old mercury! Why, I haven't even heard the word since high school chemistry! Oh, why can't Fenton leave crime to the police!"

Frank and Joe were hoping their father would call that night. To their disappointment, the phone remained silent.

"Whatever Baltimore dive he's investigating," Joe said, "he probably can't get to a phone."

"Might make a suspect suspicious," Frank agreed. Finally they turned in for the night.

They were up early Tuesday morning to get ready for their trip. Aunt Gertrude had prepared breakfast and she fussed about their eating too fast. Meanwhile, their mother packed two overnight bags, just in case they had to stay over until the next day. "Don't forget to call Jack Wayne," she reminded them.

Fenton Hardy's pilot was at the airfield and had just finished his inspection of the plane.

"Everything A-OK," he told Joe over the phone. "We can leave as soon as you get here."

The boys decided it would be risky to leave their mother and aunt alone in the house with the thugs prowling around. They contacted their friends, who all agreed to take turns guarding the Hardy home while Frank and Joe were out of town.

At the airport Jack greeted them with some disturbing news. "Two toughs have been asking questions about you. I didn't know who they were so I kept my mouth shut and they went away no wiser than when they came."

"What'd they look like?" Frank asked.

Jack described the pair.

"Snap Brim and Beret," Joe commented.

"What's that?" Jack asked.

"That's the headgear they were wearing when we first met them," Joe explained. "You see, we're real close to those two. In fact, too close for comfort."

"New case?" Jack inquired.

"Right," Frank replied. "Could their angle this morning have been to arrange an accident for our plane?"

"They might have had that in mind, but I didn't let them anywhere near it. Every working part is in order. Well, I'd better turn the engine over a few times. Warm her up for take-off. Won't take more than a few minutes."

"Okay," Frank said. "I'm rather thirsty, so I'll grab a quick cup of tea in the cafeteria meanwhile."

"I'll come with you," Joe said. "We'll meet you at the plane, Jack!"

As they were sipping their steaming tea, a voice echoed over the loudspeaker. "Calling Frank and Joe Hardy! Calling Frank and Joe Hardy!"

They looked at each other in surprise. "What do you make of that?" Joe asked.

Frank shrugged. "Let's go find out!"

They hastened to the desk and were informed that Mr. Marks wanted them to meet him at one of the airport repair shops. The clerk gave them directions.

"So Dad finally surfaced and right here!" Frank said. "Wonder why he picked this place."

"I was there with Jack Wayne once," Joe replied. "He told me that it's hardly ever used in the morning. At this time it should be vacant."

"This could mean two things. Either this is on the level and Dad doesn't want to be seen, or it's a neat little trap set up by our two buddies."

"Let's proceed with caution," Joe advised as they approached the shop. No one was in sight. Frank slowly opened the door. There were power tools in one corner; drills, auger bits, and screwdrivers along the wall.

"Mr. Marks?" Frank called out.

"Sh! Over here, Frank!" came a whispered reply.

The boys walked inside. Parts of a dismantled engine lay on a broad workbench. Crates stood piled up behind it. There were no workmen in sight.

Suddenly Frank and Joe had visions of roman candles going off, followed by an explosion of blinding light. Then they blacked out!

CHAPTER V

The Missing Missile

A VOICE that seemed to come from far off said, "Frank, Joe, wake up!"

Groggily Joe opened his eyes. The repair shop came into focus. So did Jack Wayne, who was squatting on his heels and shaking him by the shoulder.

"Boy, whoever clouted you on the head really did a good job!" the pilot said as the boys came to. "You both were unconscious when I found you!"

"You can say that again," Frank groaned. "The place seemed empty when we came in. Somebody whispered 'Over here,' and it sounded just like Dad. Then, *pow!* The building caved in on us."

Joe rubbed the back of his head gingerly, wincing when he touched the bump caused by the blow. He rose unsteadily to his feet, bracing himself with one hand on the doorknob. "I didn't see anyone, either. I'd swear we were mowed down by a runaway jetliner! Whoever sapped us must have been hiding behind the door."

"And he, or they, laid you two out like a couple of iced mackerel," Jack observed.

"We walked right into that trap," Frank said ruefully. "Should have known better. I bet Snap Brim and Beret never left the airport after talking to you, Jack."

"Sure. They sneaked around here, baited the trap with that bogus message from L. Marks, and knocked us out," Joe added.

"They must have been pretty sure you'd fall for it," Jack went on. "Who's L. Marks, anyhow?"

"An alias Dad used," Frank explained.

"Well, that's how I found you," Jack said. "The desk clerk told me that you were paged by Marks, who asked you to meet him in the repair shop."

"One thing is certain," Frank said. "They know about Dad. His cover is blown. We must alert him right away!"

"But we have no way of contacting him," Joe pointed out. "We'd better get on with the Washington assignment and hope for the best."

The boys discovered that their jackets were missing. A search of the repair shop failed to turn them up.

"We're minus our wallets, money, and driver's licenses," Joe lamented.

"We'll have to call Chief Collig," Frank said.

They all went to the administration building, where they telephoned police headquarters.

Collig took down the details. He promised to have his men comb Bayport for the thugs who had knocked the boys out.

"Meanwhile, what do we do for money?" Frank asked after he had hung up.

Jack Wayne came to the rescue. "Don't worry about financing your expedition to the Pentagon. I'll loan you the money. And there are a couple of jackets in my locker that you can borrow."

Wayne cashed a check, then the three boarded the plane. Receiving the green light from the control tower, Jack gave her the gun, zoomed down the runway, and lifted the nose into a perfect take-off. Smoothly the aircraft gained altitude. The pilot locked the automatic controls.

They flew over Baltimore. Frank and Joe looked down at the Maryland city, wondering whether their father was still there.

Their speculations came to a halt as Jack brought the plane down to a smooth landing at the Washington airport. While he stood by, the Hardys hailed a taxi and rode to the Pentagon.

A naval officer escorted them to Admiral Rodgers' office. A model warship stood on a bookcase. A multicolored map of the Pacific hung on the wall behind the desk.

The admiral was in uniform with a row of service stripes on his sleeve. He had fought in many battles on the high seas without flinching. But now he looked worried!

He asked the Hardys to tell him all they knew. Joe gave a rapid account of his attempt to put through a call to New York City, only to find that he had dialed incorrectly and had reached an office in the Pentagon.

Frank related the sound of scuffling, the call for help, and the reference to the Super S data. "And then," he added, "there were those mysterious words about the Bombay Boomerang!"

Admiral Rodgers listened with a grave expression. "You've stumbled into a real-life drama here at the Pentagon," he said. "Happened down the hall in the office of Commander Wenn, who's been directing secret research on our latest missile systems."

"Was he the one who answered our call?" Joe asked.

"Yes. He was still on the line when the intruders appeared. Luckily he had a split second in which to press a button underneath the edge of his desk. This triggered a tape recorder in a false bottom of one drawer. We've got a tape of everything that was said, including what you heard."

"What happened then?" Frank inquired.

"Someone bashed the commander over the head, knocking him out. They ransacked his office. Looked as if a tornado hit it. Drawers overturned, locks broken, files rifled, official documents strewn around like confetti!"

"Wow!" Frank exclaimed.

"The worst part is that they found what they were looking for. You heard Commander Wenn's shout about the Super S data. Well, they took it! And that is what's got us in a serious jam!"

"But what does it all mean?" Joe was baffled.

"The Super S is the newest addition to our missile program. Air-to-ground. This one zeros in on heat. The instrumentation is sensitive enough to be set for any degree of temperature above the level of lukewarm water. You probably know from your scientific experiments in high school that precisely equal degrees of heat are rarely found together outside the laboratory. The Super S will ignore every heat level except the fraction of a degree it's programmed for."

The admiral ran his fingers through his hair. "Virtually nothing can fox this missile," he concluded. "The target is a dead pigeon the moment the pilot launches a Super S."

"Are we the only nation who has it?" Frank asked.

"We used to be," Rodgers said grimly. "We'll run into international competition if those thieves smuggle the information out of the country, though! I could mention a number of foreign powers that would be interested in a deal at any price!"

"Is that what the thieves are planning, sir?" Joe inquired. "I mean, selling the information. Does the tape indicate that?"

The admiral frowned. "No, it doesn't," he replied slowly.

Frank pursued this line of questioning. "What about the phrase Bombay Boomerang? Joe and I could swear that we heard it mentioned."

"You did," the admiral told him.

"It could mean that India is involved."

"It could."

"What else is on the tape, Admiral?"

Rodgers held up one hand. "Sorry. I'll have to flag you down on that question. Can't give you the answer."

"Why not, sir?"

"Because it's classified information. No one has security clearance on the missile program except those directly assigned to Super S research."

The Hardys' expressions showed that they were keenly disappointed. They were depressed that they had made the trip to Washington, only to find the riddle as perplexing as ever.

"Don't be so dejected," Admiral Rodgers went on. "You both know what it means to be sworn to secrecy, don't you?"

Frank and Joe nodded.

"You've proved yourselves in helping your father with some difficult cases. I have some information for him which I will give you now. But it's strictly confidential."

The boys took the oath binding them to secrecy. Then the admiral proceeded.

"We've been trying to keep the lid on a very serious situation we're faced with. A Super S missile has been stolen from the Baltimore arsenal!"

Frank and Joe gasped. "How could anyone make off with a rocket belonging to the U. S. Navy?" Frank exclaimed. "It seems impossible!"

"It happened," the admiral said dryly. "Now here's what I want you to do. Tell your father, but under no circumstances anyone else. And you must speak to him personally. Don't say anything over the telephone."

Frank nodded. "Yes, sir."

"I have no opportunity to contact him myself," Admiral Rodgers went on, "since he is working underground. But I want him to get in touch with me as soon as he can."

Admiral Rodgers escorted them to the elevator. "Let me know if your father discovers any leads that tie in with this affair. It's a race against time. If we don't recover the missile, it might change the balance of power in the world!"

Frank and Joe thanked him, the elevator doors closed, and they were on their way out of the Pentagon.

They hastened back to the airport and put in a

call to the Baltimore hotel where Fenton Hardy had been staying. Joe asked if L. Marks had returned.

"Yes, he has," the clerk replied. "He left a message for two fellows named Fred and Jim. They're to meet him here. Are you Fred or Jim?"

"Jim. Thanks." Joe hung up. "We're in luck!" he exulted.

Frank was not ready to celebrate yet. "I hope you're right. But this could easily be another phony. Remember what happened to us last time we answered a communication from L. Marks?"

"Do I?" Joe probed the tender spot at the back of his head. "How could I forget, with this bump? What do we do now?"

"We go to Baltimore," Frank decided. "Only we'll be more cautious about walking into anybody's parlor."

Joe grinned. "The resident might be the spider in this case!"

"Right. The point is, we can't simply ignore the message. If Dad really left it for us, we'll have to see him. Besides, he might be in a tight corner."

Frank and Joe described their plan to Jack Wayne, who offered to help. En route to Baltimore they got down to details. Jack would remain at the airport, ready to take off at a moment's notice.

Frank said, "We have no idea where this mystery will end. Boston could be our next stop, or Miami!"

"We'll let you know what's cooking when we discover what those crooks have on their menu," Joe added.

When the plane landed in Baltimore, they had a quick bite to eat. Then Jack ensconced himself in a chair with a newspaper, prepared to sit it out until the call to action. The boys gave him the address of the hotel so he could start a search if he did not hear from them within three hours.

"Good luck!" Jack called to them as they left.

Frank and Joe hailed a taxi and settled back for the ride into town. The driver guided his vehicle through the streets with a practiced hand, weaving in and out of traffic, swerving around pedestrians, and timing his speed to catch the green lights block by block.

A big black sedan roared up abreast of the cab at top speed. "That guy sure is in a hurry," Joe observed.

The driver of the car pulled sharply to the right, cutting in front of the taxi. Frantically the cabby twisted the steering wheel to avoid a collision. He lost control as the black car forced him off the highway.

The cab careened wildly into a dead-end street! As it slewed around, the rear end slammed toward a telephone pole with terrific force! The Hardys braced themselves for the crash!

CHAPTER VI

X Marks L. Marks

THE tires of the cab screeched against the curb. Frank hung on grimly, and for one split second he got a look into the black car.

The two thugs from Bayport! Almost subconsciously, his mind registered the license plate number as the sedan shot past. Much good it would do him if the taxi wrapped itself around the telephone pole!

The vehicle bounced off the curb, shook violently, teetered sideways on two wheels, jolted to a stop and fell over just short of the pole.

"Couple of inches more, and we'd have been goners!" gasped the driver, pale with fright. Bracing his feet against the steering wheel for leverage, he forced the front door upward and scrambled out. Frantically he wrenched open the back door.

"You guys all right?" he inquired of his passengers, who had been dumped in a heap on the bottom side of the cab.

"All right would be an exaggeration," Joe grunted. "Let's say shaken up, with cuts and bruises, but hopefully no broken bones. How about you, Frank?"

"I'll live," Frank predicted.

Just as the boys were climbing out of the taxi, a couple of motorcycle policemen roared to the scene of the accident. The usual formalities of name-taking began.

"H-a-r-d-y," Frank spelled out.

"Any relation to Fenton Hardy the detective?" the officer asked.

"We're his sons."

The cabdriver, turning livid as his indignation mounted, gave a graphic description of what had occurred. He was delighted to hear Frank report the license number of the black sedan.

One of the policemen immediately pulled out a list of stolen vehicles from his pocket and ran a finger down the numbers. "Here it is!" he said.

A little while later another officer arrived in a squad car with the information that he had found the car itself with open doors, abandoned in an alley close by. No sign of the men.

"Something funny about this whole business," he said slowly, after hearing the boys' story. "Let's go over and give this car the once-over before we tow it in."

While the police examined the sedan, Frank and Joe stood by silently. Finally, just as the tow truck was driving up, Frank inquired if they might have a look inside. The officers nodded permission.

The boys saw nothing of any interest and were turning away in disappointment when Joe caught sight of a white fleck at the edge of the front floor mat.

"Just a minute. There's something under the mat." He pulled out the slip of paper.

"Takes an amateur to teach us our business," snorted one of the policemen and took it.

"Beginner's luck, Officer," Frank suggested.

"Beginner's bad luck, seems to me," the policeman retorted with obvious satisfaction after examining the paper. "You're Frank Hardy, aren't you? Well, this is a driver's license. Take a look."

Frank gulped. "It's mine!"

The boys knew they were on the spot. Since their jackets and wallets had disappeared in Bayport, they lacked any proof of identification. They were unknown to the Baltimore authorities, and all the evidence so far pointed to a connection with a car theft.

"Whatever you're up to, you've got some tall explaining to do," the officer warned them. "We'll have to book you if you don't come up with a believable story fast!"

"Will you believe Fenton Hardy?" Joe put in.

"Sure. If he were here!"

"To begin with," Joe explained, "we told the

truth. He's our father. Furthermore, he's working on a case here in Baltimore. If you'll just take us to his hotel, he'll vouch for us."

The tow truck started moving, pulling the stolen car behind. Since there was nothing more to be learned at the scene of the accident, the police decided to take Frank and Joe down to headquarters. There they were placed in the custody of a plainclothes detective for the ride to Mr. Hardy's hotel.

They drove in an unmarked car. "That's a rough neighborhood," the detective explained. "No sense in alerting everybody in sight to the fact that the law is coming."

The car swung into a heavily industrialized area, past grimy smoke-blackened factories and shoddy businesses. Here and there a delicatessen or a supermarket catered to customers with more money to spend than those who frequented the dingier shops.

The car nosed through the toughest area of all, down near the docks. Waterfront characters loomed in doorways, talking loudly. A rolling gait often betrayed the sailor. The varied accents of the foreign seamen indicated that their home ports ranged all around the world from Singapore and Liverpool, from Marseilles and Calcutta.

They stopped in front of the hotel where Fenton Hardy was supposed to be staying. Joe looked at the tacky, run-down place. "How does such a beat-up establishment stay solvent?" he wondered.

Entering the hotel, they advanced to the desk. The clerk was a handsome fellow, with dark skin and a profile of classic regularity.

He greeted the strangers with his palms together and an ingratiating smile. "What can I do for you, gentlemen?"

"Looks like a native of India," Frank thought.

The detective came right to the point. "We'd like to see Fenton Hardy."

"Fenton Hardy? I don't recognize the name. He can't be staying in this hotel unless my memory is playing tricks on me. Let me see what the ledger has to say." He ran his finger down a page. "No, just as I thought. There's no such name here."

Frank and Joe exchanged glances. They had forgotten to tell the officer that their father was not using his real name on this assignment.

Now they were really in a bind. What would the authorities think of Fenton Hardy and L. Marks being one and the same man? What would happen if the oily-mannered clerk put two and two together?

Still the truth was the only way out.

"Have you an L. Marks registered here?" Frank asked anxiously.

As the desk clerk re-examined the ledger, Joe drew the detective aside and gave him a quick account of his father's alias.

The clerk looked up. "I'm very sorry," he declared with a smirk that seemed to contradict his apology. "There's no L. Marks staying in the hotel either. Shall I search for yet a third name that may be of interest to you?"

"No thanks. We'll try for three another time." The detective turned away from the desk. "Okay, there's nothing more to be gained down here," he said to the boys. "We'll go back where we came from and start all over again."

Frank and Joe were completely discouraged as they climbed silently into the car. Suddenly Joe had an idea. "Admiral Rodgers!" he exclaimed. "Why didn't we think of him before? We just saw him at the Pentagon. He could vouch for us!"

"Maybe you know the president, too," the detective replied sarcastically.

"Look, we're not kidding," Frank protested. "Will you at least call him?"

"Sure. I've got a hot line to Washington."

By the time they arrived at police headquarters, they had persuaded the officer to put in a call to the Pentagon. Frank and Joe listened breathlessly to the conversation that followed.

The detective stated his case, then there was a brief pause. "Yes," he continued. "Let me see now. You say Frank is eighteen years old, dark hair and brown eyes. . . . And Joe Hardy is seventeen, blond hair and blue eyes. . . . Yes, the other details check out. . . . You want to speak to Frank? . . . Here he is."

The elder Hardy talked briefly with the admiral. Then he returned the phone to the detective, who thanked Rodgers for his help and hung up.

"You're off the hook," he said. "Admiral Rodgers gives you a clean bill of health. You can go now. And give your father my regards when you see him. We appreciate the work he's been doing."

"Dad'll be pleased by your compliment," Frank replied. "He's a former member of the force himself."

Leaving headquarters, Joe reflected that they still did not know why L. Marks was not registered at the hotel.

Frank nodded. "But there's a catch to that. We only know what the clerk told us. Remember, he was the only one who looked into the ledger. He never pushed it across the desk so we could see for ourselves. How can we be sure he was telling the truth?"

"I'll bet my money the other way around. He didn't look the type to inspire confidence, anyhow. What's next?"

"A look at the ledger!"

They phoned Jack Wayne at the airport, and asked him to stand by until the next day. "We intend to find out whether Dad is in that hotel or not, but we should be back by the afternoon."

Returning to the dock area, Frank and Joe staked out the hotel from a small, all-night diner,

"Look at this!" Frank whispered excitedly

conveniently situated across the street, hoping for a chance to slip unnoticed into the hotel. It was a long wait.

They could see the desk clerk from where they sat and it seemed he was a permanent fixture. Not once did he move away. Just as they were about to give up, two seamen arrived in search of lodgings for the night.

It was now or never. The Hardys watched the clerk, a different one from their Indian friend, produce the ledger to be signed. Then he reached for keys and escorted the men to their room.

This was the opportunity the boys had been waiting for. They hurried across the street, slipped through the door, and walked to the desk. Frank pulled the ledger over and opened it. Frantically he flipped the pages to the current list of guests.

"Look at this!" he whispered excitedly. He placed his finger on an entry where the name of L. Marks was inscribed in their father's handwriting! A large X was scrawled in the margin beside it!

The sight of the X mark chilled them. But they had found the information they were after and had to get out before they were discovered.

Hastily they replaced the ledger. They had taken only a few steps toward the door when a harsh voice booming across the lobby stopped them short.

"I saw you!"

CHAPTER VII

Desperate Dive

"Looks as if we've had it!" Joe muttered. "He probably saw us looking at the ledger!"

"Let's not hit the panic button!" Frank replied guardedly. "Keep cool, and we'll try to talk our way out of it!"

The boys wheeled around and walked back to the desk, feeling uncomfortable under the beady eyes of the clerk, who obviously was determined to question them about their actions.

"I saw you!" he repeated. Then he added reproachfully, "You should have waited a minute or two when you discovered there was no one at the desk. I had to show two men to their room. There's one vacancy at the moment. Do you want it?"

Frank and Joe needed all their self-control to avoid giving themselves away. What a relief! He had not spotted them at the ledger after all! Now to put up a bold front before he became suspicious.

"Yes," said Frank to the clerk, "we'd like a room for the night. My partner here is Jay Mackin, and I'm Roy Bard."

They signed the register, paid in advance, and were shown to a room.

Joe sat down on one of the twin beds. "Thank goodness we pulled that off safely!"

Frank nodded. "The thing is, we're really in the lion's den now. This place may very well be the hideout of the gang we're after, and they wouldn't think twice about rubbing us out."

"I wonder what's become of Dad," Joe mused.

"For all we know, he's somewhere in this building. Maybe he's being held prisoner!"

"That X opposite the name L. Marks in the ledger convinced me that Dad's not among his greatest admirers," Joe agreed.

Frank stared out the window into the dimly lighted street. A car horn broke the stillness with a raucous blast. Four tipsy sailors staggered past, bellowing a sea chanty at the top of their lungs.

The elder boy took in the scene before answering. "You won't get any argument from me. This hotel gives me the creeps. And we're cut off from the outside world. There's no telephone in this room, no way to contact the police."

"Right. We're a couple of sitting ducks wondering when the hunters are going to begin taking potshots at us."

The boys, tired and worried, put their heads together in the hope of coming up with a plan. Nothing practical suggested itself.

"Let's sleep on it," Joe proposed. "We can't do much until we find out who's in the hotel, and what kind of shenanigans are going on. These beds will probably give us nightmares," he concluded, feeling the lumps in the mattress before snapping out the light.

In spite of this prediction, he was soundly asleep when Frank shook him by the arm.

"What's up?" Joe inquired, with closed eyes.

"Wake up. Hurry!"

"What time is it?"

"Four A.M."

Joe groaned. "That's not a fit hour for man or beast to be up and around!"

"Quiet!" Frank whispered. "Some funny business is going on next door. There was a heavy thump—shook the room and woke me up. Then a sound as though wheels were being rolled over the floor. One of them needed oiling because it squeaked. Listen!"

Low conversation and a scuffing, thumping sound could be heard through the flimsy wall. Obviously something heavy was being moved.

By now Joe was wide awake. "Holy catfish! Sounds as if they're disposing of a body!"

"Maybe yes, maybe no. We'd better find out for sure."

The two threw on their clothes. Stealthily they opened their door a crack in order to have a clear view down the length of the hall. Moments after they took up their vigil, the door to the other room opened.

A man came out, glanced around to see that the coast was clear, and motioned to someone inside. A second man emerged, pushing a hand truck on which was a large wooden cask.

Gingerly, as quietly as the creaking floorboards would permit, the pair maneuvered it down to the end of the hall, where they squeezed it into a rickety service elevator.

As soon as the sliding doors closed, the boys tumbled out of their room in a headlong dash for the stairs. They went down the steps three at a time. Panting, they pulled up at the bottom.

"Quick!" Frank pointed. "Let's get behind that stack of laundry baskets and see what happens when they get down."

The elevator indicator moved down to number one. The doors opened. The two men eased their hand truck out, still balancing the cask on it.

One picked up the handles and began to push the burden toward the back entrance of the hotel. The other guided the carrier, while keeping a hand on the cask to prevent it from rolling off.

Silently, carefully, the boys followed. A dusty

pickup truck was parked in the back alley. Tilting the hand truck forward, the men raised the cask to an upright position so each could get a grip.

Straining and swearing under their breath, they levered the cask up into the rear of the pickup, bolted the tailboard, then climbed into the front seat. The motor came to life and the truck started to move.

"Come on," Joe hissed. Rushing forward he managed to get a foot up on the bumper and propelled himself into the back of the vehicle. Frank was right on his heels. They crouched behind the cask, hoping fervently the driver would not see them in his rear-view mirror.

The truck, gathering speed, moved rapidly through empty streets in the direction of the harbor, rattling the cask against the metal it was standing on and jouncing the boys up and down every time the rear wheels hit a bump.

Finally the driver stepped on the brake, slowing the truck on an oil-soaked dock where the water lapped against the pilings ten feet below.

"Come on," Frank whispered in Joe's ear. "Let's beat it out of here before they get wise to us."

The boys sneaked one at a time over the tailboard, dropped lightly to the dock, and dashed round the back of a nearby dilapidated shed.

"Wow!" puffed Joe, "that was pretty close. But I don't think they noticed anything."

Frank was peering cautiously round the corner of the shack. "They're unloading the cask," he reported. "Now they're rolling it to the edge of the dock."

There was a loud splash.

"They've dumped it into the water!" Frank said.

This task accomplished, the two men ran back to their truck and roared off without a backward glance.

The Hardys raced to the spot. "There it is," called Joe, pointing excitedly. "It's sinking fast."

He was right. As the cask went under, a cloud of air bubbles began to rise to the surface from around the edges of the lid!

"Somebody or something's inside," Frank said in alarm. "And maybe still alive!"

There was no time to debate the situation. Both boys kicked off their loafers and hit the water in a desperate dive.

Plunging downward, they arched underneath the cask, took hold of the bottom rim on either side, and hoisted it to the surface. With some effort they maneuvered the bulky cylinder so that it lay lengthwise on the water.

"If we can get it over to that boat slip before it sinks we'll be lucky," gasped Frank. "Let's swim behind it and try to push it and keep it afloat at the same time."

They soon had the cask bobbing toward shore.

Despite the green slime that covered the slip, they managed to get it out of the water.

"Let's stand it upright now," Frank said, grunting with effort as he proceeded to do so. "Anything we can use to pry the lid off?"

Joe crawled up the slope from the water's edge and returned triumphantly with an iron bar he had found in a pile of rusty junk on the dock.

"This should do the trick," he told Frank as he applied the bar to the rim of the cask.

The lid snapped off and clattered on the concrete. Eagerly the boys peered inside.

Slumped in a heap, seemingly unconscious, was a man in a rough tweed jacket, corduroy pants, and battered brogans.

"Dad!" Frank cried out. "Is he still breathing?"

"Yes, he is," Joe answered quickly. "Look, he's beginning to come round." He tugged at their father's arms. "Here, help me lift him out."

As gently as they could they eased Mr. Hardy out of the cask and carried him up to the deserted dock. There they slapped his face and chafed his wrists until his breathing became stronger. The color returned to his cheeks. He began to struggle feebly.

"Dad! It's us!" Frank whispered into his ear. "Don't worry, the thugs are gone!"

It took the detective a few minutes to realize that he had been rescued by his own sons. "In the nick of time, too," he said weakly. "Good work, boys. However did you know I was here?"

"We didn't," Frank said. "It was pure luck." And they told their story.

Then they turned the bulky container on its side and rolled it completely over. One stave bore the legend *Quantico Quicksilver* in heavy black letters.

"I'd call that a clue," Fenton Hardy declared with satisfaction. "Quantico Quicksilver is a major chemical company that has been losing mercury flasks to thieves!"

Frank dubiously looked at the cask. "Any point in preserving this memento?"

"No. Better put it back in the water before the thugs notice it lying around."

The boys carried the cask to the edge of the dock, depressed the open end to make sure it shipped water, and allowed it to sink out of sight. The lid, which had no markings, would only float if tossed in, so Joe kicked it behind some packing cases.

Daylight was breaking, bringing sailors and longshoremen down to the docks to assume sea duty or handle cargoes. Soon the whole harbor area would be as busy as a beehive. "Let's go," Mr. Hardy said.

They walked back to the hotel, keeping to the side streets, and discussed their next move. Slinking into the back alley, they climbed up the fire escape to the window of the room from which the cask had been taken.

They flattened themselves against the wall and listened eagerly for sounds from inside. Several men were stirring around. Spoons clinked in coffee cups. Cigar smoke drifted through the slightly opened window.

The talk was audible to the three eavesdroppers.

"Who would have thought Marks was Hardy?" gloated one of the men. "Good thing we tapped his phone or we might never have got on to him. He sure knew how to use those disguises. Only the last one didn't work!"

"Rest his soul in the briny deep," another said with a laugh. "He'll never know about the Super S now!"

CHAPTER VIII

Hotel Hideout

THE Hardys, clinging to the wall outside the window, exchanged baffled glances. The Super S again! What could these hoods know about the missile that had disappeared from the Baltimore arsenal?

The men in the room were, they knew, members of the mercury gang. They seemed to be common thieves, clever at stealing the flasks of liquid metal, but hardly important enough to put a scare into the Pentagon!

There was the flat thud of a fist against flesh and the sound of a heavy body falling against the door.

"Don't mention that, you fool!" snarled a voice menacingly.

"Why not?" came the sullen retort, presumably from the recipient of the blow. "With Hardy out of the way, there's nothing for us to worry about! We're in the clear again!"

"Oh, yeah? Suppose the Feds pick up where the gumshoe dropped out of the case? Do you want them to put us on the run?"

"If you're so concerned," sneered the other, "just tell us how the Feds could have heard my remark about the subject we're not supposed to mention! I checked this room for bugs myself. Even if they knew we were here, they couldn't tune in!"

A string of oaths greeted the protest. "You talk here, you'll talk where it isn't quite so private. So shut up!"

A third voice broke into the row. "Lay off, you guys. We've got to get on with the timetable. Dumping Hardy among the fish was only the beginning. We're moving into high gear as soon as we get the green light from Mr. Big!"

There was the scrape of a chair, then he continued. "Orders are for us to meet here tonight. Break it up for now. You've got jobs to do. I'll lock the door."

The Hardys quickly slipped down the fire escape into the alley. Finding the service elevator conveniently empty on the ground floor, they crowded in and soon entered the boys' room.

Frank was seething mad. "They tapped our home phone! That's how they knew you were Marks, Dad!"

Mr. Hardy nodded. "That's one thing I didn't expect." He started to take off his soggy clothes and continued, "My strategy worked perfectly at the start. Finding that members of the gang were staying in this hotel, I arranged to have an accidental meeting with them. We happened to be in the elevator together, and I happened to have a light when one of them brought out a pack of cigarettes."

"Accidentally on purpose," Joe mused.

"Right," his father said. "I managed to make them think L. Marks was a gangster. They assumed I was hiding out from the police and needed a job. Which impressed them favorably, of course!"

"I'll bet," Frank said with a grin.

"They were pretty close-mouthed at first, but it didn't take me long to figure out that the ringleader—whoever he is—had indoctrinated his strong-arm squad effectively with the need for secrecy."

"How did you manage to break the ice?" Joe asked.

"By bragging about being a candidate for public enemy number one, I gained their confidence. The chances were beginning to look good that they might let me in on the deal.

"I'm almost sure I was on the verge of a breakthrough when they bugged our telephone. Obviously they wanted to keep tabs on me. And what they found out was that I was L. Marks!"

Mr. Hardy paused to take a shower. When he

came out of the bathroom he rubbed the back of his hand across his forehead and took a deep breath. The effects of his ordeal showed in dark circles under his eyes. He lay down on the bed while the boys cleaned up, then continued his story.

"I had a hunch that they were on to me, so I checked out of here and returned later in another disguise, trying to find out what they knew about L. Marks. But the entire case blew up in my face last night. Two of the thugs barged into my room. They shouted that the game was up, told me they were holding you prisoners, and threatened that I'd never see you again unless I gave them my entire dossier on the mercury case!"

"Did you?" Frank asked.

"I had no choice. They had me cornered by sheer weight of numbers. Besides, they showed me your jackets and wallets."

Joe described how they had been stolen at the Bayport repair shop near the landing field. "I couldn't understand this bit of petty thievery at the time," he said. "Now it makes sense. They wanted to be sure you'd play ball."

"They couldn't have kidnapped us at the airport very easily," Frank went on. "Not with all those people around. So they tried a different gimmick, pretended kidnapping!"

"Which served their purposes almost as well," Mr. Hardy pointed out. "They got what they really wanted—the information I had gathered on them."

"Then what happened?" Joe inquired.

"Well, they had no motive to keep me alive and every reason to get me out of the way. They knocked me out, stuffed me into that cask, and took me to the harbor on a one-way trip. Luckily you two showed up in time!"

The Hardys pondered their next move.

"We're in better shape than we were before," Frank commented. "Those thugs are convinced that they've disposed of Fenton Hardy. Okay, we'll play it their way! Let them continue to think you're dead, Dad. They won't be suspicious that anyone is on their trail, let alone closing in on them. Could be they'll become careless."

Joe was excited by Frank's strategy. "Since they don't know we're in the same hotel with them, this is the perfect hideout for us. We're their next-door neighbors. So we'll be able to keep an eye on them."

"An ear too," Frank added with a chuckle. "It shouldn't be too difficult for us to bug their room!"

"That's a problem," Mr. Hardy put in. "Those hoods took my electronic equipment. We'll have to retrieve it somehow."

Frank spoke up. "I'll go down and arrange for another night in this room. It would be embarrassing if our hideout were suddenly pulled out from under us because we neglected to pay the bill!"

"And while you're downstairs, how about picking up some food?" Mr. Hardy suggested. "I'm famished! Haven't had anything to eat since noon yesterday!"

Frank took the elevator down to the lobby. The day shift had not taken over yet, a big relief to him since he preferred to avoid the Indian of the previous afternoon. The night clerk willingly agreed to let "Mackin" and "Bard" occupy their room the following night, and Frank paid up.

Then he sauntered out of the hotel and into the diner across the street. He ordered a stack of sandwiches along with cartons of steaming hot coffee and was soon back in their room.

The sandwiches diminished rapidly under the onslaught of the three Hardys. The coffee disappeared just as quickly. They all felt better as they put the debris into the wastebasket. The detective was beginning to be himself again.

"A couple of hours' sleep and we should be as good as new. That's all we can afford if we're to keep the gang under surveillance."

"I think one of us had better stand guard in case anyone tries to break in," Joe suggested.

"Good idea."

Joe volunteered to stay awake since he was not

particularly tired at the moment. While the others turned in, he stationed himself in a chair near the window.

Turning over the pages of a magazine, he listened to the sounds of the hotel coming to life. The buzz of cars in the parking lot indicated that the day shift was replacing the night shift. The elevator clanged as guests arrived and departed. A low hum of voices from the street reached the room.

Suddenly footsteps approached along the hall. Two men stopped at the door of the Hardys' room, conversing in an undertone. "Shall we go right in?" Joe heard one ask.

He stiffened. "The enemy is preparing to charge!" he thought. "Better summon reinforcements." He stepped around the bed to wake his father. Then he paused.

"There's no point in going in there," the second man declared. "That's not our room. We're on the floor below."

"That's what comes of going on a bender just off the ship!" replied his comrade with a hiccup. "Come on. Let's go down before my legs give out. I'm gonna snooze the clock around!"

Joe relaxed and went back to his chair. "This kind of interruption I can do without," he murmured. He allowed his father and brother to catch up on their sleep, and roused them at the time agreed upon. Both were ready for action.

"Anything happen while we snoozed?" Frank wanted to know.

"Nothing but a false alarm, although it gave me quite a turn," Joe told him, and went on to describe the incident of the sailors in the hall.

"It's good you took note of them," Mr. Hardy said soberly. "From now on, we have to be extra careful of those we're dealing with. Regard everyone who approaches as a suspect until he clears himself. We'll cover our tracks—"

A pounding on the door cut him off. Mr. Hardy's voice sank to a whisper. "I can't be seen here when you're the only ones registered. If you need help, yell!" With that he disappeared into the closet.

"Who's there?" Frank called out sharply. "What do you want?"

Joe slid silently behind the door, prepared to jump anyone who tried to force his way in.

"It's the desk clerk," stated the man outside. "You guys gotta get out, we need the room!"

CHAPTER IX

A Bug on a Wire

"WHAT are you trying to pull?" Frank demanded. "We've paid in advance so we could stay in this room for another night!"

"Too bad about that," said the surly voice. "But there's been a mistake. We had an earlier reservation the night clerk didn't know about. Another party's coming in. So you'll have to vacate!"

Frank played for time. "Okay, we'll pack our things and get out of here. But how about another room in the hotel? After all, we're paying customers, cash on the barrelhead!"

"Nothing doing. Every room is occupied. My orders are to get you out before check-out time. Nothing personal, you understand. Just business."

"Okay, we'll be off the premises by noon. However, you've still got the money we've paid in advance. If we don't get it back pronto, you'll have to carry us out!"

"Don't worry, wise guy," growled the clerk. "You'll get your dough—right now!"

There was a rustling sound as some dollar bills appeared under the door. Frank stooped and picked them up as footsteps retreated down the hall.

"Better see if it's all there," Joe said.

"It's all here," Frank said cheerfully, flipping the bills with his thumb. "They're only too glad to pay off. Which means they want to get rid of us with as little fuss as possible."

Now that the coast was clear Mr. Hardy emerged from the closet. The three held a council of war about what to do next.

"We'll have to work fast and pick up as much information as we can before noon," Mr. Hardy said.

"Think there's anything in that story about an earlier reservation?" Joe asked. "The man who came to our door didn't sound like the day clerk we met yesterday."

His father shrugged. "Perhaps. It could also be that they want to clear the hotel of any outsiders."

Frank sighed. "Well, it's all in the game. We can't take anything for granted."

"What now?" Joe asked.

Fenton Hardy gave Frank and Joe a rundown on the main facts of the case. The evidence he had collected before being discovered pointed to a high-power conference of the gang that night. And what they had heard on the fire escape proved it.

"We ought to sit in on their session," Joe observed. "By remote control. How do we get our bug back, Dad?"

Mr. Hardy looked thoughtful. "Those thugs who put me in the cask took it. Before they knocked me out, I saw one of them place my electronic equipment in a closet. If we can only get into their room, we should be able to find it easily enough."

"In other words, it's time for us to see if anyone's home!" Frank chuckled.

The hall was empty. The Hardys walked quickly to the room next to theirs where the thugs were staying. Frank tapped on the door. He was sure no one had returned, but was prepared to ask for a fictitious person if anyone answered, and then pretend that he had made a mistake in the room number.

The subterfuge was not necessary. No sound came from within. Frank tried the knob. "Locked, of course," he stated.

His father took a long needle-sharp gadget from his pocket to pick the lock. Meanwhile the boys stood guard on either side, looking up and down the hallway, keeping a nervous eye on the elevator, ready to give instant warning if anyone appeared.

Mr. Hardy worked with deft speed. "This one's a cinch compared to most I've opened in my career," he said softly.

Then he stood up, turned the knob, and pushed. The door swung inward, revealing an untidy scene. Bedclothes were piled up where they had been thrown aside, cigarette butts were scattered on the floor, an overturned coffee cup had spilled its contents on the table.

Fenton Hardy did not have to explore the room. Quickly he walked to the closet, opened it, and felt carefully along the shelf. "Here it is!" He brought down the coil of wire with the metal sphere on one end and the receiver on the other.

"Everything okay?" Frank queried anxiously, poking his head into the room.

"Yes. They may have intended to use the bug themselves. If so, they'll have to postpone that plan because we have a prior claim."

Mr. Hardy closed the closet. "Let's get out of here!"

As Frank looked around the room, his eyes rested on a newspaper on the table.

"Dad," he murmured, "over there—the *Bayport Times!*"

Mr. Hardy picked it up. "That's strange. I wonder why they brought it all the way to Baltimore." He stuffed it inside his shirt. "We'll take it along and catch up on the news back home."

They quickly left the room. Mr. Hardy closed the door, jiggled the knob to be sure the lock had slipped back into place, then led the way to the elevator.

"Now where are we going?" Joe asked.

"We haven't much choice. I'd say the roof," Mr. Hardy replied.

They stepped out of the elevator on the top floor, climbed a narrow flight of stairs, and arrived at a skylight door. Frank pushed it open and they went onto the roof.

"This seems our best hideout," Mr. Hardy said, looking around.

"Might as well get set for a long siege," Frank added. "Our friends aren't due back until this evening."

They found a corner where the projecting skylight cast a long shadow across the roof, agreed that this was a good vantage point, and sat down to rest and wait.

Mr. Hardy pulled the Bayport newspaper from his shirt. Frank and Joe looked on from either side as he flattened it out.

"Hm! Nothing on page one to interest us," the detective commented. "Or have I overlooked something?"

"Not as far as I can see," Joe answered. "Maybe there's a clue on the inside pages."

They carefully scanned the paper, remarking on stories of the Bayport scene, but found nothing that had even the remotest connection with the case.

Mr. Hardy said, "It's unlikely that there's anything in the radio and TV section. But let's check."

Joe whistled as he looked at the first page. "Hey, what have we here?" He placed a finger at the top of the program listings where somebody had drawn a red pencil circle.

"That's our local kilocycle number for Bayport radio," Frank said. "The station plays hit tunes nearly round the clock as you can see from the program. What's the name of the disk jockey again, Joe?"

"Teddy Blaze. He's only been with the network a short time, I believe."

"What do you make of this?" Mr. Hardy inquired.

"Beats me," Frank replied.

"Why the thugs would be interested in popular music is a mystery to me," Joe added.

When darkness fell, they carried their electronic bug to the parapet. Mr. Hardy readied the receiver while Joe cautiously payed out the wire over the edge until the instrument dangled outside the thugs' window.

Soon it began picking up sounds of the gang congregating inside. Feet scuffled. Chairs creaked. Voices buzzed. Bits and pieces of conversation came through.

"Now that Hardy is out of the way," someone declared, "we can get on with the job of heisting the empties."

Frank and Joe looked blankly at their father as if asking, "What empties?"

He shrugged, indicating that he was as mystified as they were. Nothing in the talk going on down below enlightened them. Obviously the gang understood the reference without having the details spelled out.

The discussion shifted to topics that the Hardys already knew about. They were beginning to doubt that they were going to hear anything useful, when suddenly an authoritative voice issued a warning that made them prick up their ears.

"I want you guys to get this through your heads! Button up your lips about the Bombay Boomerang! We're too close to the big play to let anything go wrong now! The whole deal could be ruined if the cops get wise to what we're up to."

Breathlessly the Hardys waited for him to continue. Were they finally going to learn about the Bombay Boomerang?

So intent were they on the conversation down below that they failed to notice the rising breeze. It caught their wire, with the tiny bug dangling on the end, and wafted it against the windowpane in a series of sharp taps!

The window went up with a thump. A head peered upward. "Someone's on the roof!" a voice

Joe cautiously payed out the wire

yelled. "Get up there quick!" Chairs scraped and fell over as the entire gang jumped up and pounded through the door.

There was no time to lose. Desperately the Hardys sprang to close the skylight door. What could they use as a barricade? Only a master TV antenna was on the otherwise empty roof. Frank and Joe ripped it down, jamming its metal rod against the solid tin door, using the parapet to anchor the other end.

Just in time! The first gangster up the stairway was banging against the door with his fist. Those behind cursed and shouted, telling him to keep going.

The Hardys were trapped! No sense trying to climb down the fire escape with the thugs so close behind. There was only one desperate chance. They would have to leap across the alley to the building next door!

Mr. Hardy went first. Gathering speed as he ran he leaped onto the parapet and sprang into space. The boys gasped in relief as he landed squarely on the other side.

Frank followed, using the same technique. Then came Joe. But when his foot touched the parapet, seeking leverage for the jump, it slipped. He could not stop himself and knew he would never clear the distance. Below him lay a solid six-story drop and the hard pavement of the alley!

CHAPTER X

The Disk Jockey's Dog

DESPERATELY Joe threw his arms forward! His fingertips clutched at the edge of the roof, and he hung there, straining every muscle. He knew he could not last for more than a few seconds. Already his grip was beginning to weaken. He slid back toward destruction!

"Hold on, Joe," Frank yelled.

Rushing to where Joe dangled helplessly, Mr. Hardy and Frank grabbed him by the wrists. Hauling frantically, they got him safely up on the roof.

"Thanks," Joe panted. "I hope that's my last cliff-hanger!"

"We'd better get out of here before we have company," Frank warned, pointing toward the opposite building, where by now the barricaded door started to give.

They hastened to a skylight door leading downstairs. Luckily it was unlocked. With Mr. Hardy in the lead, they lost no time in getting to the elevator.

"I hope it doesn't stop on the way," Joe said nervously.

"If we're delayed, we might have to hide out in the building," his father remarked. But the elevator went straight down and they hurried to the front door.

"Keep your cool," Mr. Hardy warned under his breath. "We don't want to arouse suspicion."

Frank peered outside. "The coast is clear," he reported. "And—wow! We've got help! Jack Wayne is just getting out of a red Ford over there!"

"What timing!" his father exclaimed. "Let's make for Jack's car!"

Walking briskly across the street, the fugitives reached the Ford, jumped in, and crouched down on the floor. Frank peeked through the rear window.

"I don't see the hounds yet. The elevator next door must have stopped on every floor," he said.

"What about Jack?" his father queried.

"He went into the hotel. Probably got worried about us."

Joe rose slightly to get a view of the hotel entrance. "Oh, here they come!" he warned. "Duck low!"

Four men barreled out of the door. Two ran in opposite directions. The other two plunged into the alley and continued right around the building.

They met again, shrugging in obvious disappointment, and began to argue furiously. Finally they dashed into the building where the Hardys had just been.

Jack Wayne emerged from the hotel accompanied by the desk clerk. They, too, were in the midst of a heated dispute, the pilot insisting that the Hardys must be there, the clerk just as certain they were not.

"If Frank and Joe cleared out, they'd certainly have let me know," Wayne stated vehemently. Getting nowhere, he broke off the discussion, returned to the car and jumped in.

Frank tapped him lightly on the shoulder. Startled, Jack wheeled around.

"Easy, Jack," Fenton Hardy whispered. "All three of us are here. Act as if nothing has happened and make tracks for the airport, quick!"

Catching on, the pilot whipped the car out of the parking spot and maneuvered it skillfully through the traffic.

The Hardys relaxed. "That was simply beautiful, Jack," Frank said. "Where'd you get the car?"

"Borrowed it from a fellow I know at the airport," Jack replied. "Since you didn't call, I thought I'd better check up on you. What happened?"

"Nothing, really," Joe said. "We just had to make a rather unorthodox exit. Our friends at the hotel didn't want to let us go!"

Soon the airport came into view. Mr. Hardy's plane stood on a side runway. He went straight to it.

"We'll wait inside," he said. "Gives us more privacy than the lobby. Jack, do me a favor. Call Captain Stein at police headquarters and have him come out here if possible."

"Sure thing, Mr. Hardy." Jack strode into the administration building. Only ten minutes after his return the captain arrived.

Fenton Hardy briefed his colleague on the current status of the mercury case. The captain whistled.

"We had no idea the affair was that big! Murder, eh? We'll have to look into that!"

"I'd like to see two steps taken right away," Mr. Hardy replied in grave tones. "To begin with, the hotel should be placed under surveillance at once. At least three or four plainclothesmen, considering the size of this gang. We don't know who the leader is yet, but one of his henchmen might lead us to him."

"Right." Captain Stein scribbled a few lines in his notebook. "And then?"

"If you could spread the word to the news media that Fenton Hardy of Bayport has disappeared under mysterious circumstances it would help. Add that no clues have turned up, and that the case appears to be running into a dead end."

"I get you," the captain declared, snapping his notebook shut. "When those guys read the story in the Baltimore papers, they'll be more sure than ever that they're safe. You'll have a better chance to find out what they're up to, since they won't be looking for you!"

"That's the idea, Captain. I'm glad you approve of it. Makes me feel more secure."

"Sure thing, Mr. Hardy. We like to have you on our side, too."

"Well," Mr. Hardy said, "I'm flying back to Bayport with Frank and Joe. We have some clues to follow up."

It was the middle of the night when Jack Wayne set the plane down at the Bayport airport.

"Before we go home, I want to make a call," Mr. Hardy said. "It's not the best hour to phone Admiral Rodgers, but I have to talk to him."

The admiral brushed aside an apology for waking him up. "My sleep is of no consequence when national security is concerned," he said. "What have you to report?"

Fenton Hardy said as much as he could over the phone and proposed a secret meeting in Pittsburgh the following evening. Admiral Rodgers agreed.

Then the Hardys returned home to an affectionate welcome from Mrs. Hardy and Aunt Gertrude.

The next morning Frank and Joe held a get-together with their friends. Nothing out of the ordinary had occurred at the Hardy house during their absence, the boys reported.

"If anything had happened," Joe said, laughing, "I'm sure Aunt Gertrude would have informed us the moment we stepped in the door."

"We've come up with another problem," Frank said. "What do you know about that disk jockey Teddy Blaze?"

"He's considered a groovy character," Biff related. "Puts on platters with a real beat. The kids at school are wild about his program."

"One thing bugs me about him," Chet offered. "He's forever chattering about his dog. Tells us his canine companion is named Balto, and then talks to him over the air. Weird kind of nonsense you can't make out."

"Chet, you may just have given us a vital clue," Frank said. "Balto—it's worth checking out. Come on, Joe! Let's see what we can find out at the newspaper office!"

They located the radio and TV critic in his cubicle writing a review of a Bayport jazz concert.

"What do I know about Teddy Blaze?" he replied to their question. "Not much. He's new around here. Comes from somewhere in the South. Maryland, I think. Anyway, the kids go for him in a big way. If you're after personal information, you'd better go see Teddy himself. He'll be at the studio now."

Frank and Joe thanked him and had no difficulty getting into the studio when they announced they were fans of Teddy Blaze. The disk jockey had left orders that his fans were to be admitted.

"Good publicity," said the doorman with a wink.

The boys found Blaze in top form, or as Joe put it, "flip and insufferable!"

"You fellows look like refugees from the Bach brigade," he gibed. "Are you beginning to see the light? Does my music provide you with spiritual sustenance?"

Frank was nonplused. "That's not the kind of patter I expected," he thought. "Hardly the lingo of the hep generation."

Joe took up the disk jockey's line. "We've switched. But I imagine we're not the only ones in these parts. You must have a lot of fans."

"You're coming through loud and clear," Blaze boasted. "But modesty forbids me to tell you the size of my listening audience. Ask my press agent. He'll be less humble about it."

The man gave the visitors a sidelong glance and asked slyly, "How's your famous father? I'd have given him the big hello if he'd come with you. I dig his detective methods!"

Joe put on a long face and said glumly, "Haven't you heard? Dad's disappeared. Took a trip to Baltimore and hasn't been seen since. Very mysterious!"

Blaze seemed hardly distressed to hear it. "Any suspicions?" he inquired in a somewhat mocking tone. "Any idea of what could have happened to Bayport's celebrated sleuth?"

"Plenty of suspicions," Frank answered, "but they don't seem to lead anywhere. Perhaps we'll have news about him later. I don't really want to talk about it. Let's get to the music!"

"We came down to the studio to discuss your program," Joe added. "It's for a paper we have to write in school. How do you pick the platters you play on the air? Intuition?"

"Not entirely," Blaze replied smugly. "Intelligence might be a better word. Look here. This is a list of the disks that are selling best around the country. I know what my millions of fans are going for each week, and I give it to them."

While Frank deliberately kept the disk jockey engrossed in his own cleverness, Joe walked around the room, looking at pictures and records. Then he leaned behind a filing cabinet, holding a record from the stock lying on the table. He removed an envelope from his pocket. Making sure that Blaze's back was toward him, he scattered some fine powder over the center of the record where the man had braced his thumbs to avoid smudging the grooves.

He blew the powder aside, revealing a perfect thumbprint. Guardedly he brought out his miniature camera and snapped a picture of the print. "If there's anything on Blaze in the police files, this should do the trick," he thought.

Replacing the record, he rejoined his brother and Blaze, who were debating the merits of two combos that had recently performed in Bayport.

As the Hardys took their leave, Blaze remarked maliciously, "I hope you find your father. It wouldn't do for his brilliant sons to be foxed on a case where the missing person happened to be the famous man himself!"

Frank and Joe pretended to be downcast at the thought. They hurried from the studio as the disk jockey returned to his records and his fans.

The boys went straight to the office of Chief Collig, where Joe brought out the film of the thumbprint from Teddy Blaze's disk.

"I'll have it developed right away," Collig agreed, "and do an immediate check to see whether it matches one in our files."

Driving home, Frank suggested that they listen to Blaze's program. Joe fiddled with the knob until he got the right kilocycle. A pop tune came bouncing through the radio. As it ended, they heard Blaze's voice:

"Hello, out there! Ready for an afternoon of the sweet and cool with a dash of hot syncopation? That's what you want, and that's what I've got for you. And now to my dog Balto. Are you listening? The next number is dedicated to Flatfoot and the Flunkies. You don't believe it? How suspicious can you get? Plenty. Sock it to 'em! Right up here in Bayport. That's the ticket!"

Joe snapped the radio off. "Is that stuff supposed to be groovy?" he growled.

CHAPTER XI

Patter in Code

"I don't think Blaze is trying to be groovy," Frank responded with a thoughtful frown. "That kind of talk sounded to me more like a riddle."

"You mean a code? Secret information for listeners who know how to decipher it?"

"Why not? Look, what do you make of Flatfoot and the Flunkies?"

"Dad and ourselves!" Joe exclaimed. "I'll bet that's it! Balto must stand for Baltimore. He's telling his confederates in Baltimore that you and I are suspicious about Dad's disappearance!"

Frank shifted gears and turned into their driveway. "That's how I figure it. The rest fits in, too. When he mentions socking it to 'em in Bayport, that could be an order for his pals to deal with us!"

"But we can't be sure that's his game after hearing him on the air only once. Let's have his program monitored while we're in Pittsburgh. Chet and the others will probably be glad to oblige. I'll give them a ring."

Their friends were enthusiastic. They liked Blaze's recordings. And they vowed to listen in turn to his patter in the hope of breaking the code, if there was one.

That settled, the Hardys were preparing for their trip when Chet Morton's car drew up in front of their house, wheezing and backfiring as usual.

Joe was puzzled. "We just talked to him over the phone. Wonder why he's coming to see us."

"He must have bounced over here as fast as his motorized tin can would travel," Frank replied. "We'd better go out and see what's bothering him."

Chet's car was standing at the curb. The driver sat at the wheel, fiddling with the ignition.

Joe called out, "Chet, what's up?"

"That's not Chet!" Frank shouted the warning. "Duck, Joe!"

Too late! A man hiding in the back of the car leaped out. Leveling a spray gun at them, he fired its contents into their faces. The liquid burned and stung. Frank and Joe staggered back, temporarily blinded by the assault.

"There's more where this came from," snarled their assailant. "Pull out of the merc racket while you've got time! Stay on our backs, and you'll go

the way your old man went! We're through fool-
ing with you!"

Before Frank and Joe could open their eyes to
get a look at the pair, the car had roared off. The
boys soon recovered, agreed that they had been
the victims of a variety of tear gas, and returned to
the house. After a thorough soap-and-water wash-
ing, they consulted their father about the incident.

The phone rang during the conversation. Chet
was calling. "You know what's happened?" he
queried glumly. "My car's been stolen. My pride
and joy is in the hands of thieves!"

"We've just seen it," Joe told him. "In fact, it
was borrowed for a visit to Frank and me." He
described what had happened. "Report the theft
to the police, Chet. They should be able to locate
it easily. There aren't many cars like it around.
And tell them that it was used for shooting gas
into our faces. I was just about to call Chief Collig
myself."

Chet phoned later to say that his jalopy had
been found. "The thieves abandoned it near the
bay. The crime lab people examined it, but found
nothing incriminating."

"No clues at all?" Frank questioned.

"No. Chief Collig says the guys were pros who
didn't leave any calling cards. Not so much as a
fingerprint. So he still has no lead to the mercury
gang."

Mr. Hardy decided that leaving from Bayport for Pittsburgh might be too risky, so he and his sons drove to an airport several miles away. Jack Wayne had flown in to pick them up, and they were soon in the air.

When the Golden Triangle at the confluence of the Allegheny and the Monongahela showed up in the distance, Jack cut his engines, made a big circle, and came down for a landing on instructions from the control tower.

Then he went into the administration building, while the Hardys rented a car. "We're to rendezvous with our friend at the third motel right down this highway," Mr. Hardy explained. "Place called Vacation Inn."

Frank made the turn at the neon sign. The motel was an oblong structure with rooms along three sides. They parked and went directly to the room where the admiral was waiting. It was in the middle of one section, so the get-together would be as inconspicuous as possible.

The officer was dressed in civilian clothes when he opened the door. "Another precaution," he informed the Hardys. "My naval uniform would stick out like a sore thumb in this place."

He motioned Frank and Joe to sit down on the sofa, while Mr. Hardy made a quick search for hidden microphones. Then the admiral went right to the heart of the matter.

"This Bombay Boomerang angle has me

stumped. At the Pentagon, we've played the tape from Commander Wenn's office over and over. With regard to that phrase, we literally don't know anything yet."

He glanced at the two boys. "I hear you fellows are experimenting with boomerangs, so maybe you have a theory."

Frank shook his head. "Nothing yet, sir."

"My secretary did some research, and she said the weapon is native to India as well as Australia. Does that tidbit lead us anywhere?"

Frank shrugged. "Where it leads—if it leads anywhere—I don't know. But your secretary is right, Admiral. The Indian boomerang isn't as famous as the Australian version, but many Indian families cherish their boomerangs as heirlooms and even as sacred relics."

"Our expert, Chet Morton of Bayport, says that in olden times Bombay was the metropolis of the southern India boomerang country," Joe put in.

"India keeps popping up in this case," Frank noted. "Remember that Indian desk clerk in Baltimore. He's been one of our suspects ever since we saw him. And—"

Mr. Hardy held up a warning hand. "*Sh!* Someone's outside the door!"

A key eased into the keyhole. The individual trying the lock twisted it gently at first, then with greater force as it stuck. He was determined to get into the room.

Admiral Rodgers strode to the door. Flinging it open, he surprised a man bending over and fumbling with the key.

"What do you want?" the admiral barked.

"I want to get into my room. What are you guys doing here? This is number 69, isn't it?"

"No, it's 89!" The admiral's tone showed his annoyance at the interruption.

The man was plainly embarrassed. "Sorry," he stammered apologetically. "I didn't mean to intrude." He retreated toward number 69.

"An honest mistake, I believe," Rodgers said, rejoining the circle. "But it's enough to give one the jitters when strangers crash into a conference like this."

"We can arrange to keep them away," Joe declared with a grin. "At least honest ones!" Stepping over to the door, he hung a "Do Not Disturb" sign on the outer knob.

Mr. Hardy picked up the thread of the conversation. "I believe the vital question concerns the relation between the mercury case and the missing missile. What can they possibly have in common? If we knew that, we'd have the solution."

"There's another mystery that might link the two, although right now I don't see how," Frank said. He and Joe reported their suspicion of Teddy Blaze, the artist of the disks.

They stressed their belief that his patter contained coded messages for his confederates.

"Anyway," Frank continued, "we may soon have a break on this angle. Joe took a thumbprint from one of Blaze's records. We left it with Chief Collig to be checked out."

Admiral Rodgers was impressed by the news.

"It's a lead worth running down," Mr. Hardy stated emphatically. "There's got to be a Baltimore–Bayport connection in all this. What do you think, Admiral?"

"I agree with you. But the Indian angle also has to be considered. I've been looking into it myself. A freighter from India is docking at Baltimore day after tomorrow. The *Nanda Kailash*."

"You think she warrants investigation?" Frank asked.

"Yes. Find out what cargo she carries, what crew is handling her, and if there is anything suspicious about her voyage."

"We'll be glad to check her out, sir," Joe said.

"Fine. But I don't want everyone on the ship to get wind that an official investigation is underway. I'll arrange with the captain for you to go aboard without arousing suspicion. And you're both good detectives. Is that all right with you, Mr. Hardy?"

"Frank and Joe can take care of themselves," the detective replied. "I have every confidence that they can give the freighter the once-over, and bring back the facts."

"Okay, then." Rodgers wound up the conference. "We'll leave it at that until something breaks. You can report to me at my office. If I'm not there, call my home any time of the day or night and we can get together. This case must be solved, and judging from the Hardy record, you could be the ones to do it."

"That's a compliment, Admiral," said Mr. Hardy, "and I hope we can make it stand up. This is about as tough an assignment as I've ever been on."

Frank and Joe echoed the words of their father. "We'll do our best to beat this gang," Frank said.

Admiral Rodgers went immediately to the airport to fly back to Washington. The Hardys spent the night at the motel. Early Friday morning they left for Baltimore. They took turns driving the rented car.

Frank looked at his watch as they neared their destination. "This is one of the hours when Teddy Blaze is on the air. We might as well listen to his program, Dad. It'll give you some idea of what we're talking about. And you might pick up a clue that would get by us."

Joe flipped the radio to the Bayport station. The disk jockey was playing a popular recording, and the rhythmic beat filled the car.

"Nothing to pick up there," Mr. Hardy declared. "That music isn't my cup of tea. Guess I'm too old and far away from the younger generation to appreciate it."

The piece ended. Blaze came on with his breezy

patter. At first everything seemed in order. He was talking the jargon of the trade, using the slang of the new generation to hold the attention of his audience.

Suddenly his tone changed, and so did his patter. Through the radio came the words, "Balto says tonight is the night for a new record album "Steal My Heart Away," and it's strictly for you, precious."

"Now there's a nonsense line if I ever heard one," Joe volunteered. "That is, if it really is nonsense. You see, Dad, that's why we think there may be more to it than meets the ear."

Frank had been musing over Blaze's announcement. "Assuming that he's in with the mercury thieves, he could be telling them that a new assignment is on the agenda. He might be ordering them into action tonight. But where?"

The three discussed the possibilities in this interpretation. They were baffled when they came to the word "precious" in the disk jockey's talk.

Suddenly Mr. Hardy sat bolt upright. "I know a company in Baltimore named Precious Metals!" he exclaimed. "Can it be next on the gang's list? Will Precious Metals discover tomorrow that a shipment of mercury has been stolen?"

CHAPTER XII

Cemetery Search

"IF those thugs are planning to hit Precious Metals," Fenton Hardy mused, "then I'd better warn the company. We can't just sit on this information while they make off with the mercury."

"Well, we certainly have to do something," Frank agreed. "But suppose an employee of the firm belongs to the gang. If you phone he might get wind of what's up and sound the alarm. And he could be in management. Even if you went there in person—"

"That's right!" Joe interrupted. "They could call off the heist at the last moment and reschedule the operation for a later date."

His father mulled over the problem. "You're probably right. In any case, we should be able to keep the factory under surveillance. Pull into that service station over there, Frank. I want to phone a friend of mine."

After making the call, Mr. Hardy explained that his friend had an office in a high-rise building across from the Precious Metals company.

"He's invited us to use his premises in any way we see fit. As there's some distance between the two buildings, my idea is to rig up a telescope and watch events in the factory yard. We can buy a ten-magnification model on our way downtown."

Soon they had reached their destination. With Frank carrying the black barrel of the instrument, and Joe the tripod, they went to the top floor. Mr. Hardy's friend, who was on his way out of town, had telephoned the superintendent to unlock his office and let them in. Without wasting a minute they set the telescope up at an open window.

Training it on the rear of the factory, Mr. Hardy scrutinized the area. "This will do nicely. We'll be able to spot a single flask of mercury, and even the label. Have a look!"

Frank peered through the eyepiece. The magnifying power of the instrument made every object look enormous. Swiveling it from left to right, he took in the panorama of office buildings, warehouses, and trucking areas.

"A lot of movement going on," he said. "And a row of mercury flasks in one corner. Could they be what the gang is after?"

Joe took his turn at the telescope. "Wonder if anybody we know is working down there. Guess not, but we seem near enough to strike up a conversation. Wouldn't that driver in the green truck be surprised to learn that we've met by way of a telescopic lens!"

The Hardys had a clear view of Precious Metals until evening when rain started to fall heavily.

"No use staring into that deluge," Fenton Hardy muttered in disgust. "Our rig will be useless until it stops."

About an hour later the rain slackened off, then petered out. The three observers trained their telescope back on the factory yard, which was now empty.

"The afternoon shift has gone home," Frank observed. "The only guy left is the guard at the gate."

"Anything suspicious we should report to the police?" his father inquired.

"Maybe!" Frank answered with suppressed excitement after a short pause. "The guard is letting a truck through. It's pulling up to the mercury flasks! The men in the truck are too furtive to be legitimate. I think the robbery must be on, although the truck is blocking our view! Take a look at that, Dad!"

Meanwhile, Joe called Captain Stein. "We'll have reinforcements in a few minutes," he said as he put down the phone. "The police are on their way."

"Those flasks are heavy," Frank added. "Stealing that many should keep them occupied long enough for the U. S. Cavalry to come riding to the rescue!"

"Wrong!" his father exclaimed in startled tones. "The truck is moving already! There it goes, right through the gate! And the flasks are all gone!"

The Hardys rushed down to the street to meet the police. A rapid inspection of Precious Metals showed that the detective had been right. The thieves had gotten clean away with the mercury. There was no sign of the guard, either.

"An inside job," Mr. Hardy explained to the two police officers who had arrived with Captain Stein. "The guard at the gate was in on it. Obviously the thieves waited for him to give them the high sign. All they had to do was drive in, load the truck, and drive out. He probably went with them."

"The mystifying thing is the timing of the job," Frank declared. "Even with inside help, it should have taken much longer to steal a shipment of mercury. No one can juggle one-hundred-and-thirty-five-pound flasks as if they were empty beer cans!"

The captain shook his head. "Something mighty strange is going on here. Did you get the license number of the truck?"

"Yes." Frank handed him a slip of paper on which he had written it down.

"We'll check it out, even though I'm afraid it's

a phony." Captain Stein went to his car and reported the number over his radiotelephone. Then he rejoined the Hardys.

"Frank and Joe, suppose you get to work on this problem with Captain Stein right away," Mr. Hardy suggested. "I'll have to get back to Bayport before morning."

"Okay," said Frank. "Let's take our rig down at the office and be on our way."

Upstairs, while the boys disassembled the telescope, Mr. Hardy donned one of his numerous disguises. "Can't go back into the lion's den any other way." He grinned. A thick black wig covered his head and he pulled a matching beard and mustache out of his brief case. By the time he was finished, even his sons did not recognize him.

"One more point," he said, before departing. "Since I'll be in Bayport, I'll see what I can find out about Teddy Blaze, beginning with a visit to headquarters. The thumbprint report should be on the chief's desk by now."

Frank and Joe joined the police in searching the Precious Metals property for clues to the robbery.

"Footprints first?" Joe inquired. "After the cloudburst, the thieves couldn't have tramped across the yard without leaving some pretty good prints."

"We have a clear set right here," an officer grunted with satisfaction. He was pointing to the spot where the men had lifted the flasks into the truck. "The guy who made them was big. Size thirteen shoe, probably. Otherwise, I can't see that they tell us anything we didn't know before."

Frank was squatting down, giving the footprints a thorough inspection. "Look closer, Officer. What do you make of the depth of these marks?"

"Depth? Oh, I see what you mean. They're shallow. Those guys don't seem to have been carrying much more than their own weight."

"Yet," Frank pursued the point, "they're supposed to have been toting flasks weighing a hundred and thirty-five pounds. One flask is enough to make a man sink flat-footed in the mud!"

The policeman frowned. "Perhaps we'll have the answer when Jack here from the crime lab takes impressions. Footprints and tire marks both," he added to his colleague, who was getting out his equipment.

Frank and Joe watched as the lab man took impressions from the soft ground. "We're not the only ones interested," Frank said suddenly, cocking a thumb at a couple of sailors who seemed fascinated with the proceedings at the scene of the crime.

The seamen were Indians, each dressed in a blue jacket with a red stocking cap on his head. Their dark eyes took in the scene, flickering from the Hardy boys to the policemen, and then down along the ground where tire ruts had corrugated the earth just off the pavement.

"The Indian theme again," Joe murmured. "Do they give you the impression of being spies, Frank?"

"I haven't made up my mind on that. Anyway, they have a perfect right to watch what we're doing. No point in challenging them just yet. Better wait for them to tip their hand."

Captain Stein approached. "We've got clear impressions. Nothing more on the footprints than you mentioned before. They're too shallow for men carrying heavy burdens."

Frank nodded. "I thought so."

"The tire impressions are something else. We know that the left rear tire of the truck is worn nearly bald, far down past the treads. The right has a deep slash that's cut into the rubber almost to the inner tube. They're sure headed for a super blowout."

"That might just be the break we need," Frank said.

"Right. We're going to cruise around this part of Baltimore and look for the truck along the routes leading toward the city. Want to come along, boys?"

"Sure!" was the instantaneous answer. They climbed into the back of the car, while the three officers occupied the front seat. Back and forth they cruised, up and down the truck routes, without sighting the vehicle that Frank and Joe had watched at Precious Metals.

"Let's try the service stations," remarked the captain, "in case a blowout's occurred already. They may have called for assistance."

He cut off the highway into the first gas station. Frank and Joe got out and asked whether the attendant had received a call concerning a truck with a flat tire, but the answer was negative. They had no more luck at the next half-dozen service stations. Then Captain Stein received a report on the radio that the license number was a phony.

Finally the first break developed. One attendant told them about a call he had received from near Westminster Churchyard, at Fayette and Greene streets. A truck driver had reported that his right rear tire had gone completely. "He wanted us to give him a tow," the man said. "I told him we'd be along whenever we could, but we've been tied up with an accident along the highway. Haven't been out to Westminster yet."

"We'll take care of it," said Captain Stein, and stepped on the gas.

One of his colleagues turned and glanced at the Hardys. "As detectives you should be interested in Westminster Churchyard. The writer who invented the detective story is buried there. Edgar Allan Poe himself."

Joe chuckled. "We sure could use him on this case. It's as tough as the murders in the Rue Morgue any time!"

The patrol car swung through the city up to the cemetery. "There he is." The officer pointed to Poe monument, Baltimore's salute to the master of mysteries. "And that appears to be the truck we're looking for!"

It was the one all right. The blowout had torn the one tire to shreds, but the second fitted the impression taken from the Precious Metals loading area.

"No one inside," Frank observed. "They must have been scared off while they were waiting for a tow."

"No load, either," Joe added. "The mercury flasks are gone!"

"The crooks probably carted them off by hand," Frank went on. "If they transferred them to another truck, they wouldn't have called the service station to fix the blowout. Joe, the flasks might be stashed away not far from here!"

"The cemetery! We'd better give it a search!"

Captain Stein agreed. "Let's separate. You two go together, and if you see anything, give a yell!"

"And don't let the spooks get you," one policeman said with a grin.

"It's spooky all right," Frank muttered as they set out.

In the moonlit graveyard leaves rustled in the

wind. Tombstones cast eerie shadows. Off in the distance a dog howled.

Frank and Joe began working down from the northwest corner where the Poe monument stood, stepping carefully around the graves as they searched.

A cloud scudded across the face of the moon, leaving the cemetery in darkness. The boys waited for the brightness to return. To while away the time, Frank asked in an undertone, "Which of Poe's characters does this situation remind you of?"

"The black cat." Joe grimaced.

The cloud swept past. They resumed their search under the light of the moon. "What's that?" Frank pointed to an object, shaped like a milk bottle, near a large mausoleum.

"A mercury flask!"

They hastened around behind the mausoleum and found a pile of containers, heaped up as if they had been thrown there in a hurry.

Frank picked one up. "Hey, Joe! This sure doesn't weigh a hundred and thirty-five pounds. In fact, it's empty!"

Joe examined a number of others and whistled softly. "So are they all. The mercury is gone!"

CHAPTER XIII

Aboard the Indian Freighter

JOE held one of the flasks upside down and waited to see if any last drops of mercury would drip out. None did. He tried the same experiment on several more containers with the same negative results.

"If it had been a quick-change operation and the thieves had poured the mercury into their own containers, we'd be almost certain to find a trace in each flask. Yet these are all bone-dry."

"Of course they are. They were empty to begin with," Frank said, "which helps us to fit together two pieces of this jigsaw puzzle. First, we heard one of the gang mention 'heisting the empties.' That makes sense now. And second, the footprints at the Precious Metals loading yard were too shallow for men carrying one-hundred-and-thirty-five-pound flasks. Now we know why. There was no mercury in them."

"It must have been stolen earlier," Joe agreed. "Probably on the dock where the cargo was landed, or maybe aboard ship. The empty flasks might have been taken to throw us off the track."

"So," Frank said, "it's just as well we have an appointment with an Indian freighter. Right now we'd better tell Captain Stein of our discovery. And we'll call Dad early tomorrow morning."

The police investigated the place where the flasks had been discarded. After that, they drove Frank and Joe to a hotel, where the boys took a room for the night. Next morning they telephoned their father through a Bayport neighbor, since they were afraid their own phone was still being tapped. Mr. Hardy was puzzled by the empty mercury flasks. He said he would query other companies that handled mercury and call back.

An hour later the boys were still batting the mystery back and forth when the phone rang. Their father said that several companies reported finding empty mercury flasks. "They're baffled about the method used by this gang. You could be right in suspecting thievery on the dock or the ships. See what you can find out aboard the *Nanda Kailash* and keep your eyes open for any connection between the disappearing mercury and the Bombay Boomerang, Frank!"

"Okay, Dad. We'll go to the ship right away."

Frank and Joe took a taxi to the harbor. They

drove along a narrow street lined by large warehouses and heavy trucks to an open area dominated by the Indian freighter tied up at the dock. She was painted black, with a white band high above the waterline amidships. Derricks, slings, and lifts rose over the hold from which the cargo was being unloaded. The stern, riding high out of the water as it became lighter, bore the name *Nanda Kailash,* and underneath her home port, Bombay.

The taxi stopped at a gate where the guard told the boys they would have to proceed on foot. They saw mobile cranes handling massive bales of jute. Piles of debris covered much of the dock— broken crates, empty barrels, lumber, and other fallout of unloading activity. A big red barge, rocking at the dockside behind the freighter, was receiving part of the cargo for transportation across the harbor.

"Plenty of action around here," Joe observed.

Dark-skinned workmen from the *Nanda Kailash,* wearing navy-blue sweaters, bustled between the deck and the dock. Frank asked one how to get aboard. The man, giving them a suspicious stare, pointed to a steep metal stairway extending up the side of the ship.

"Climb we must," Frank quipped. He took hold of the white rope railings on either side and started up the steps, feeling them sway under his weight. Joe followed close behind.

They were halfway up the stairs, with a steep drop to the dock beneath them, when Frank suddenly jerked to one side and yelled, "Duck, Joe!"

His brother swung out on one railing in a reflex action. A huge bale of jute came hurtling down, barely missing them and landing on the dock with a heavy thud.

Joe took a deep breath. "Wow! Was that, or was it not accidental?"

"Your guess is as good as mine," Frank said. "Anyway, let's get up on deck before we're treated to an encore."

The long deck extended toward the bow on the right, to the stern on the left. The boys had paused to inspect a bulletin board where the names of the ship's officers were posted when a steward asked what business they had on board. After listening to their explanation, he led them down a narrow corridor to a large cabin.

"This is the chief officer's quarters," he said in a soft Indian accent. "Please sit down. I will inform him of your arrival. Would you prefer tea or coffee? . . . Coffee? . . . A few moments, please."

Frank and Joe glanced around the room. They were surprised at the degree of comfort it reflected. The paneled walls and furniture seemed to be mahogany. A couch, three chairs, and a table were covered in a gay multicolored print. One cabinet held a radio and record player.

On the opposite side of the cabin was a built-in

bunk with a drawer in its base, flanked by a desk on which lay a volume entitled *Rough Logbook*. Nautical pictures hung on the wall opposite the porthole.

"Nice pad," Joe murmured. "Life at sea must have its compensations."

The door opened. A dark, good-looking man came in. Shaking hands with the boys, he introduced himself in excellent English as Chief Officer Jal Agopal, substituting for the captain, who was ashore.

The steward appeared holding a tray with a white coffeepot, three cups, milk and sugar. Deftly setting a cup and napkin at three places on the table, he withdrew.

Jal Agopal took a sip of coffee, then inquired what he could do for his visitors. "Naturally I am anxious to aid Admiral Rodgers in every possible way," he said.

"Perhaps the first thing I should mention," Frank replied, "is an incident that happened when we were coming aboard." He described the bale of jute that nearly knocked them off the ladder.

The chief officer expressed his apologies, adding that he was as mystified as they were. "You must have noted that the cranes swing cargo over that part of the ship. But I've never known that kind of thing to happen before. I will make an investigation."

"Duck, Joe!" Frank yelled

Joe asked about the crew.

"We carry fourteen officers and thirty-six men," Agopal replied. "I'm not familiar with the personal background of each one of them. All I can say is that every man is skillful at his particular job on the freighter. If there is anything wrong, it hasn't come to my attention."

"Perhaps the cargo might give us a clue," Frank put in. "What are you carrying this trip?"

"The usual things. Tea, curios, jute, burlap, carpets—"

"Mercury, too?"

"Yes, also mercury. We loaded the flasks at the Spanish port of Cadiz."

"Where do you keep them during the voyage from Spain to the United States?"

"In the hold with the rest of the cargo. Come. I'll show you how it's done."

Jal Agopal led the Hardys out of the cabin, along the narrow corridor, and back on deck. As they walked toward the hold, Joe nudged Frank and nodded toward a sailor slinking along on the opposite side of the deck.

He was a tough-looking character in a plaid work shirt, who ducked behind a pile of crates when he realized that he had been spotted. When the boys pretended to have lost interest in him, he promptly reappeared.

"Our bodyguard," Joe whispered to his brother. "Services rendered free of charge."

They reached the hold, a yawning cavern that looked to be two or three stories deep. The men working at the bottom were shifting carpets onto hooks attached to cables that carried them in swinging arcs up to the deck and across the side onto the dock.

"Quite a lot of activity," Frank said to the chief officer.

"We have only a limited time to unload, load, turn around and meet our timetable for the trip back to India," he replied. "To you it must seem very confused. Actually, every step is precisely planned."

"I don't see any mercury flasks," Joe said.

"You will. They come aboard on trays, fifty at a time. You undoubtedly know that they are heavy, and are fastened with screw-type steel caps. As a sling lowers a tray into the hold, members of the crew lift the flasks off one by one and store them together in the hold space provided for them.

"Because of their weight, they need special attention when they reach the hold. We shore them up with wood to prevent slipping. And we do not pile any other type of cargo on top of them."

"How safe are the flasks in the hold?" Frank asked. "I mean, can the crew get at them either during the voyage or in port?"

"Oh, yes. The hold itself is open. These particular flasks have not been unloaded yet. But there is no rule that prevents the members of the crew from going down into the hold and inspecting them, as long as no one gets in the way of the men working on the docks."

The boys leaned over the edge for a better look. Men called back and forth in their native tongue. Those below signaled to the men above when to haul away. Winches, tackle, and cables strained under the weight of their burdens.

Joe stepped onto a pile of rope, paying little attention to the events on deck. Suddenly the rope tightened with a tremendous jerk as someone yanked the other end. Joe tumbled head over heels into the hold, hurtling down toward the bottom far below!

CHAPTER XIV

Down the Hatch

HORRIFIED, Frank saw his brother topple head over heels into the hold. The chief officer gasped. Crewmen shouted excitedly in Hindustani and English. But no one could do a thing to help!

Flailing his arms wildly, Joe fell like a stone. Then, in mid-air, his toe hit something. Throwing out a hand, he grabbed hold of a cable and swung himself onto a rolled carpet that was being hoisted up onto the deck of the *Nanda Kailash*.

Joe stood up shakily when the carpet hit the deck. "This kind of trip I could have done without," he muttered, managing a weak smile.

Frank was ghastly pale. "I thought we'd be picking you up in little pieces at the bottom!"

"Someone on this ship doesn't like us," Joe said, his face grim. He looked straight at the chief officer.

Jal Agopal plucked a handkerchief from his

breast pocket and wiped the perspiration from his forehead. "Thank God we were unloading carpets when you fell," he said with a sigh.

Then his gaze traveled beyond the boys to the crew. "This is an outrage!" he declared, and there were both anger and fear in his voice. "I intend to find out at once who pulled the rope that tripped this boy! If it was deliberate, he is a murderer! I want him identified!"

He ordered the entire crew to be mustered on deck. The men lined up along the railing towering over the dock. Agopal addressed them.

"Most of you must know by now of the near-fatal accident that just occurred. For those of you who haven't heard, I will simply say that one of our American guests fell into the hold because someone pulled a rope from under his feet. He managed to seize one of the cables, which is the only reason he is alive to tell the tale. If any of you have any information on this, speak up!"

A dead silence greeted the announcement. Jal Agopal spoke to a number of the men assigned to the unloading, but they all insisted that they were hard at work at the time. Even the eyewitnesses had no idea how it had happened.

Frank and Joe conversed in low tones with the chief officer, describing the individual who had been following them around the ship. Agopal invited them to inspect those on the deck, and to see if they could identify their shadow.

The boys went down the line, peering sharply into each face. At the end, they declared positively that the man in question was not there.

"He must have sneaked aboard," Frank suggested to the chief officer.

"That may well be correct," he replied with a worried frown. "This is the whole crew. Any additional personnel would be strictly unauthorized. As long as we remain in port, I will post special guards to catch this stranger if he tries to slip on or off the ship. But why would he deliberately try to harm you?"

"Perhaps he mistook us for someone else," Frank said casually. Soon after that, he and Joe went ashore. They shook hands with Jal Agopal, climbed down the swaying stairs from which they had almost been swept while boarding the ship, and made their way back to the hotel.

Soon they were sitting in their room munching sandwiches and discussing the recent events. Frank scratched his head. "The mystifying thing is how this character knew enough to follow us aboard. We didn't broadcast the news of our arrival."

"I'm with you on that. But don't forget that the mercury gang has a lot of operatives, including several who can identify us on sight. They must have tailed us, learned of our plan, and detailed an agent to arrange a rousing welcome for us on the freighter."

Frank nodded. "Rousing and final. He carried out his assignment so well that flowers would have been appropriate if that carpet hadn't come along in time to offer you a lift."

"Don't I know it! I can still feel myself going down the hatch in a perfect swan dive!"

"Then there's the question—"

Frank never got to state the question. A tremendous thump on the door brought both boys to their feet. Racing to the door, they wrenched it open and caught a glimpse of a furtive figure disappearing into the elevator.

A heavy, circular, wooden object, propped up against the door, toppled forward, tripping them up.

"This looks familiar," Joe observed as he tilted it on edge and rolled it into the room.

"It should," Frank answered grimly. "That's the top of the cask Dad was in when the thugs dropped him into the harbor. They must have found it down on the dock. Do you realize what this means?"

"This!" Joe pointed to a message painted across the wood with a spray gun. It said:

> PUNKS! SO YOUR OLD MAN IS ALIVE!
> WE WILL GET HIM, AND YOU TOO!

Joe touched the lettering with his finger. "This paint job wasn't done too long ago. It's hardly dry."

"It was probably done after your unsuccessful trip into the cargo hold. I wonder when they found the lid!"

"We'd better call Dad and tell him that his escape has been discovered."

"First let's clear out of this place or—"

Another sound at the door brought them to their feet again, ready for action. Since they had left the door ajar, they expected a band of thugs to come storming in on them. Frank seized a chair and swung it in front of him. Joe prepared to use his favorite karate technique.

A hand pushed the door wide open. Two figures stood on the threshold.

"Relax!" a familiar voice exclaimed.

"No need to break up the furniture just because we're here," said another.

Phil Cohen and Tony Prito!

Joe grinned at their pals from Bayport. "Boy, are we glad to see you! We were expecting to tango with some rather unfriendly partners."

"Including," Phil guessed, "the strong-arm pair from our home town?"

"The same. But what brings you here just when the death-defying Hardys were about to go into their act?" Frank asked.

"Your father," Tony explained. "Indirectly, anyhow. He told us he had left you here to case an Indian freighter. After we talked to him, it seemed cruel to let you handle this problem by yourselves, especially since you might be eyeball-to-eyeball with an entire gang. So we decided to give you some shock troops support."

"We can use it!" Frank said, then told his friends about the enemy's latest strike against Joe.

"Seems as if we're going to get a piece of real good action!" Phil declared.

"You might. But first tell us the latest news from Bayport. How's Chet doing?"

Tony chuckled. "We would have brought him along, but he's too busy with his boomerangs. In fact, he's such a success that he's going into business, selling them to a local hardware store. There's no lack of customers. The kids have a boomerang club, and they're tossing those things like crazy all over the landscape!"

"Not only the landscape," Phil said with a laugh. "So many of them keep whirling off-course in Bayport that the glaziers are doing a bang-up business replacing broken windows. Quite a few hats have been knocked off, too. No injuries, however, as far as we've heard."

Finally Frank called the meeting to order. "Phil and Tony, suppose you stay here in the hotel room. Joe and I will go down the fire escape to avoid any thugs who might be lurking in the lobby. We must phone a warning to Dad that his cover's been blown for a second time. Then the four of us will hold a council of war concerning our tactics. Agreed?"

"Agreed."

Frank and Joe descended the fire escape without incident, located a pay phone booth, and called their Bayport contact again. No one was home at the Hardy house, however, and the neighbor promised to pass the warning on to Fenton Hardy as soon as he returned.

The boys went back to the hotel and circled around to the rear. Suddenly Joe nudged Frank and pointed upward. A man was climbing up the fire escape toward their room! He moved cautiously, casting covert glances at the tenth-floor window.

The Hardys exchanged silent signals. Joe ran around to the lobby. Seizing the house phone, he told Phil and Tony of the approaching prowler. Frank started up the fire escape at top speed, but the man, with a long head start, reached the open window before him and edged himself through into the room.

As Frank mounted, he heard sounds of a struggle. Phil and Tony had jumped the intruder, and he was giving them a battle royal. Breaking loose, he scrambled back over the window ledge, regained the fire escape, and started down.

Only then did he become aware that Frank was on his way up to meet him. He turned to retreat up the fire escape. Frank brought him down with a flying tackle on the ninth-floor landing.

High above the street, they grappled with one

another on the iron platform. Frank's powerful adversary threw him on his back and began to pound his head against the iron grating. In a desperate attempt to break the man's grip Frank wedged a hand under his chin.

Clutched in deadly embrace the two rolled toward the edge of the landing, and toward nine stories of empty space beneath them!

CHAPTER XV

Sailor Suspect

FRANK grabbed one of the bars of the fire escape to keep from going over the edge. Wrenching himself free, he scrambled to his feet and met his opponent with a one-two combination of punches. The man keeled over backward and lay motionless.

"Cold as a clam," Frank thought. "It's good he left me that opening or I might be on a long jump to the street."

He turned to the other three who had joined him on the landing. "Let's tote our visitor inside and hear what he has to say for himself."

They carried the man into their room and placed him on one of the beds. As he gradually returned to consciousness, his body twitched and he mumbled in a foreign language. He was young, no more than twenty, the boys estimated.

They searched him and found a carved dagger of a type common in the Orient.

"He's from India," Phil observed, studying the youth's skin and regular features.

"And that must be Hindustani he's speaking," Tony said. "It's no language I ever heard."

"Correct on all counts," Joe asserted. "I've seen this man before. He was aboard the Indian freighter. Remember, Frank? He was in that line-up we inspected."

Frank pinched his lower lip thoughtfully. "Yes, I thought I recognized the face during our tussle on the fire escape. This can only mean one thing. He's in cahoots with the guy that tried to throw you down into the cargo hold, Joe. Maybe others are involved too—including our friend Agopal."

Joe nodded grimly. "I was hoping that it had been an outside job, but now the whole crew is suspect."

"You should have your answer in just a moment," Tony spoke up. "Our friend appears to be coming to."

The man groaned and opened his eyes. Obviously the four faces staring sternly down at him frightened him. He moved over to the wall before sitting up.

"Who are you?" he stammered, looking at Phil and Tony.

"Suppose you tell us who you are," Joe said firmly.

"My name is Nathoo Keeka. I belong to the crew of the *Nanda Kailash*. We finished unloading here in Baltimore and were given shore leave."

"What have you got against me and my brother?" Frank demanded. "You're going to stay where you are until you tell us the truth!"

The Indian sailor hesitated. He seemed to be debating with himself about how much he should tell. At last he spoke.

"I will tell you the truth, no matter what you may decide to do with me. There is nothing the least bit dishonorable in my conduct."

"Oh, no?" Tony exploded. "What's so high-minded about armed robbery with a dagger?"

"Robbery was not my intention," Keeka protested indignantly. "I am no thief. I am a faithful worshipper of the high god Krishna!

"You!" He pointed an accusing finger at Frank and Joe. "You are the guilty ones. You have committed a sacrilege!"

The four boys were dumbfounded.

"Come again?" Joe suggested weakly.

"You two have desecrated a statue of Krishna. For that you must be punished. I am but the unworthy instrument of divine vengeance!"

"There's a crazy kind of sense coming out here," Frank muttered, pulling up a chair. He waved the others back to give the man more breathing room.

"Now listen to me," he advised their prisoner. "That's an absurd charge. We haven't been near a statue of Krishna or any other Hindu god. Who told you that story?"

"Another man on the dock described the incident. He swore he saw you deface the image. I must vindicate the honor of the god who is sacred to me!"

"Tell us about the man who spun this yarn," Phil urged. "Who was he? What did he look like?"

"I do not know his name. He was an Indian seaman I met on the dock."

Nathoo Keeka proceeded to give a detailed description of a man in a plaid work shirt who had set him on the trail of the Hardy boys.

"The sneaky character aboard ship!" Frank burst out. "The one who followed us around the *Nanda Kailash* and yanked that rope that tumbled Joe into the hold!"

"You mean he is an enemy of yours?" Nathoo asked in amazement. "He insisted that he had no interest in you personally. He was concerned, he said, about nothing except punishing you for the sacrilege you committed."

"Why didn't he punish us himself?" Joe inquired.

"He told me he was not a Hindu."

"Then why does he want to avenge a Hindu god?"

Nathoo Keeka looked troubled. He folded his hands across his chest. "I see that I have been grossly deceived. My profound apologies to both of you. It is fortunate that you stopped me. I shall offer no resistance if you wish to summon the police to take me to jail."

The boys held a hurried consultation. Believing the story, they decided to be lenient with their unexpected visitor.

Frank spoke for the group. "Don't worry, Nathoo. Your explanation has convinced us that this is not a case for the police. Instead of prosecuting you, we'd like you to help us."

"I will be glad to do anything you say."

"The sailor who deceived you is a criminal. You don't want him to go free, do you?"

The seaman shook his head.

"Neither do we. But this thing is bigger than one man. A gang is involved, and we could use another hand to help break it up."

Frank gave Nathoo a general account of the mercury thefts. The Indian quickly grasped the problem. "Mercury? My freighter often carried cargoes of it. I have helped load and unload the flasks many times. Not as easy as you might think. They are heavy."

"That's right," Joe agreed. "But they seem to lose their weight somewhere between the ship and their destination. That's why we would like your cooperation."

"How? I am merely a sailor aboard the freighter. How can I possibly help solve an American crime?"

"We're not so sure that it's strictly American. Anyhow, we have to start at the spot where the stuff comes into the country. It would be extremely useful if you could keep us posted regarding events aboard ship, so we can follow the mercury from the moment it is being unloaded."

Keeka seemed doubtful. "Wouldn't it be better to have the help of one of the officers?"

"Not at all," Frank replied. "We need a man who can mingle with the crew and the workmen on the dock."

"You fit the bill, Nathoo," Joe urged. "Besides, you know one member of the gang. You might find a lead there. How about it?"

Nathoo Keeka reacted to the plea with a simple word. "Okay!"

After a minute he continued, "My country and yours will be better off for the capture of these criminals. And I will have the satisfaction of settling my account with the deceiver who hoped that I would murder you!"

Frank stood up. "That's fine, Nathoo. Here's your dagger. Now let's get out of here."

Since the Hardys had paid in advance, they did not have to go to the lobby. The five climbed through the window and descended the fire escape. Walking rapidly through a maze of streets and alleys, they headed for another hotel. Frank was sure they had not been followed.

All the while the boys kept up an animated

conversation with their new friend. It had nothing to do with crime or criminals, but with the fascination of India.

"I'm interested in the god Krishna," Phil declared. "Tell us more about him."

"The great god Krishna," Nathoo Keeka intoned gravely, "is the deity who preserves the universe. He is the hero of our epics. He is the teacher of kindness and brotherhood. You can see why he is so important in Hindu religion. The life of our people would be entirely different if we did not worship the mighty preserver of all things."

Frank cast a glance at the Indian's serious face as he continued:

"I was obeying our commandment against sacrilege when I tried to kill you. If you had really been guilty, I would not have felt a twinge of remorse!"

Tony felt slightly uncomfortable at Nathoo's last statement and changed the subject with a quip.

"When I think of India, I have visions of tigers and elephants and maharajahs. That's what I'll be looking for if I ever go there!"

Nathoo Keeka laughed. "Tigers and elephants are there in the jungle. The maharajahs still exist, even though they are not as powerful as they used to be. My friend, come to India and we will hunt the tiger together!"

Joe mentioned the Taj Mahal.

"Ah, there you have our masterpiece!" Keeka declared. "The Taj Mahal in Agra, built by the Great Moguls, who invaded India. But then, so much in our country was put there by invaders.

"My home city Bombay was only a small fishing village a few centuries ago. Then the British came. They needed a big seaport to handle merchantmen from Europe, and Bombay provided the site."

Frank judged this the right moment to spring a surprise question on their informant.

"What do you know about the Bombay Boomerang?" he asked sharply.

"Why, we have plenty of boomerangs in Bombay. The people of southern India used them for hunting. Today, however, they are mainly considered objects of art, sacred relics, and cherished heirlooms. Antique dealers do a thriving business in them, especially to American tourists. Our—"

"I'm not talking about boomerangs in general," Frank interrupted. "I'm talking about the Bombay Boomerang."

"Bombay Boomerang? I don't know what you mean. No single weapon has a special place in our tradition." Nathoo stopped and broke into a grin. "Perhaps you refer to the *Bombay Batarang?* That is another freighter en route from India. She will dock at Baltimore this afternoon!"

CHAPTER XVI

Boomerang or Batarang?

THE boys gaped in astonishment. They had been convinced that Bombay Boomerang was the phrase that had come through the phone in Commander Wenn's office.

Was it possible that the words had been *Bombay Batarang?* the Hardys wondered.

"What's all this boomerang stuff about?" Phil inquired.

"Just a phrase we picked up. Thought it meant something," Frank replied.

He pulled Joe aside and they let the others go ahead. "What do you make of this?" he asked.

"Don't know. Admiral Rodgers, too, is sure that the intruders said Bombay Boomerang."

"That was before we heard about the ship," Frank countered. "Maybe the Pentagon tape should be checked again. Suppose the gang intends to slip the Super S on board the *Batarang* for a trip out of the country?"

"We don't have time to go back to the Pentagon, not with the freighter docking here this afternoon. Let's check out the *Batarang* as soon as she comes in."

"Since there are five of us, we could divide forces, one group to go aboard, the other to patrol the docks," Frank mused.

"Right. But remember, all this is classified information. We can't tell the others much about it."

"They don't have to know the details," Frank decided. "And we can give them a general idea of what we're after."

They found a suitable hotel and checked in. Then Frank called a conference and outlined their plan. Phil and Tony were eager and ready for action, and Nathoo Keeka spoke up excitedly.

"I can help. I have friends on the ship. We could visit them."

Joe was enthusiastic. "That's great, Nathoo. I'll go with you."

"Me, too," Phil volunteered.

"Fair enough," Tony said. "Three on board and two ashore. That leaves Frank and me to patrol the docks. Suit you, Frank?"

"Sure thing. Nathoo knows the ship and we'll familiarize ourselves thoroughly with the docks. That way we should get a pretty good idea of what's going on."

The five went down to the dock to acquaint

themselves with the area, streets, warehouses, fences, and the ships at anchor.

"Not much doing on Saturday afternoon," Frank remarked. "Wonder who's responsible for that eyesore." He pointed to pile of junk. "Look at that Chevy. Vultures sure have done a job on it. Not a door or a wheel left."

"Not even a window," Joe added. "Well, there's the *Bombay Batarang* at the pier. We'd better go aboard."

"Don't forget," Frank warned, "that you three are to rendezvous with us here on the dock this evening. If you don't show up on time, we'll have to assume that you've run into trouble and come for you. Maybe we'll even call the police."

"Why don't you give us more time?" Joe asked. "Let's say till the early-morning hours. We might be able to find out something by talking to the crew when they're off duty tonight."

"Okay, let's make it dawn," Frank agreed.

Joe, Phil, and Nathoo walked across the dock toward the *Bombay Batarang*. Behind the freighter a red barge bobbed up and down on the waves. Stevedores were busy transferring jute into the barge, moving the huge bales through side doors that gave access to a deep, dark interior.

The three climbed a steep ladder, with Nathoo Keeka in the lead.

"Here's hoping no one throws a bale of jute at us this time," Joe thought, recalling the narrow brush with death he and Frank had encountered while boarding the *Nanda Kailash*.

One by one they stepped onto the deck of the freighter. From the opposite side of the ship came the loud clang of hammers beating on metal.

"What's that noise?" Phil asked.

"Members of the crew knocking the rust off the hull," Nathoo explained. "But allow me to describe the layout of the freighter before anyone interrupts us. After all, we might get separated, in which case you should know where you are on the ship and how to get off by the most expeditious route.

"The first deck—the one on which we are standing—has the chief officer's cabin, much like the one on the *Nanda Kailash*. The second deck has the captain's cabin."

"Probably the nicest accommodations on the ship," Joe remarked.

Nathoo grinned. "The third deck," he went on, "is of the utmost importance because that is where the chart room and the bridge are located. I know the first mate in charge of navigation. His name is Ram Giga."

He led the way up to the third deck via a series of metal stairs. Continuing on toward the bow, Nathoo and his companions reached the chart room.

This was a narrow cubicle with a high built-in worktable. Books on navigation and maps on the

Atlantic coastline were scattered across it. The log told the daily story of the voyage from India. The echo sounder on one side indicated the depth of the water under the ship.

The two officers in the room looked up as the visitors entered. One was Ram Giga.

"Welcome, Nathoo!" he said with a wide smile. "Who are your friends?"

Nathoo introduced Phil and Joe and asked for permission to spend some time aboard the vessel.

"We will be glad to have you," Mr. Giga replied.

His colleague, Assistant Engineer Luckman Kann, wore a sour expression. He seemed irritated by the arrival of strangers, and kept giving Joe and Phil venomous looks.

Ram Giga, an affable individual, willingly answered a few questions.

When Joe asked about cargo, Giga replied, "We have a hold full of many items for American-Indian trade."

"What about mercury?" Joe asked.

"Part of the cargo is mercury. We will deliver it to the dock as soon as we can get it out of the hold. It is due to be carried off this evening."

Joe and Phil had the feeling that Luckman Kann resented the chief mate being so free with information. "The mercury is only part of the cargo," he declared harshly. "You may be more interested in some other things we are carrying, ivory statuettes and similar curios from the Malabar Coast, for example."

Joe and Phil quickly agreed, in order to dispel any suspicion about their visit.

Ram Giga, ignoring Kann, went on, "We're late in unloading due to the dock strike that just ended. Usually we would have the mercury off by now, but the rest of the cargo had to come first. The men are working overtime tonight to get all the cargo ashore. Now I must get back to my duties. You are welcome to look around."

"Is this wise?" Luckman Kann grumbled. "They will only be in the way!"

"I will amend the invitation, then," Mr. Giga said mildly. "You may move around the ship freely as long as you do not interfere with the unloading."

"Thank you. We will be most careful not to disturb the labor," Nathoo assured him.

Motioning to Joe and Phil, he led them out of the chart room to the bridge, where he explained the technical gadgets.

"The high seat you see is for the pilot. The wheel may seem small to you, but it is the ship's brain, transmitting directions that maintain a true course. The gyrocompass next to it gives the bearing so that the navigator can be sure of his direction."

"What's that orange dial in the low metal housing over there?" Joe asked.

"Radar. I cannot imagine how sailors ever made a safe voyage without it."

Phil examined a large wheel equipped with a handle to turn it through the various positions around a circle.

"That is the telegraph," Nathoo said. "Sends orders regarding speed to the engine room."

"Better not spin it, Joe, or you'll have the engine room on the phone asking what's happening on the bridge," Phil remarked jokingly.

Nathoo went on, "The small windows along that circle belong to the smoke indicator. Each window is connected to a vent from a different part of the ship. In case of fire, smoke is sucked into one of these holes and one can tell where the fire is. But we have seen enough here. Let us go down to the engine room."

The three stood on oily catwalks, high above the throbbing engines. Narrow, slippery steps led down to the floor. After looking around for a while, Nathoo said, "We better stop sightseeing and get on the job."

"Right," said Phil. "Let's go back to the deck." He was in the lead when they climbed up again. They made their way through a maze of passages until, on reaching the third deck, Phil suddenly realized that he was all alone. Joe and Nathoo were gone!

He went down again, but could not find them. "No point wasting time looking for them now," he told himself. "I'll have another look at the bridge. We might have missed something the first time around."

Finding the bridge empty, he began to examine the navigation instruments once more. That was the last he remembered. A heavy blow on the head knocked him unconscious, and he collapsed against the telegraph!

CHAPTER XVII

Precious Wreck

SLOWLY Phil regained consciousness. He heard voices conversing in a low key. He felt a wet cloth on his face, and the hard floor on the bridge underneath him.

Opening his eyes, he saw that several officers were grouped around him. As they swam into focus, he realized that one was the captain of the *Bombay Batarang*.

Phil got to his feet with the assistance of willing hands. "What happened?" he asked weakly.

The captain placed a hand on his shoulder to steady him. "Do not be too concerned about what happened. The main thing at the moment is to be sure that you are all right. I am having you moved to my cabin to recuperate."

"Someone hit me over the head!" Phil declared.

"Yes. With a blunt instrument. In falling, you struck the telegraph handle, spinning the wheel and alerting the engine room to the fact that something was wrong on the bridge. I rushed up here and found you lying in a heap. You have a headache?"

"Awful," Phil replied, and everything began to spin again.

While he was being put to bed in the captain's cabin, Frank and Tony were on a back street, maintaining surveillance from a doorway about a block from the piers. All had been quiet as far as they could tell.

"Not a suspicious character in sight," Tony complained. As he started to walk away from the doorway, a truck lumbered slowly up the street.

Frank seized Tony's elbow and pulled him back. "That truck is similar to the one that hauled away the empty flasks from Precious Metals!" he said tensely. "We've got to find out whether this one is carting mercury!"

The truck rolled to a stop across from the doorway, at a spot where the pavement widened out along a fence with a gate nearby. Frank and Tony peered across the intervening distance, to see if they could spot a mercury flask.

Two men got out of the truck and opened the tailgate. Using a block and tackle, with a winch for power in leverage, they lifted their load into the air, swung it out of the back, and deposited it on the pavement. Releasing the hooks, the men swung the block and tackle back into place and returned to the front seat. Then they drove off.

Frank and Tony watched the whole procedure in utter amazement, for the load was the wreckage of what once had been a car. Like the Chevy they had seen earlier on the dock, this hulk had been stripped clean of every usable part. Motor, wheels, fenders, lights, doors—all were gone. Little more than a skeleton remained, battered metal that seemed hardly worth the attention of a junk dealer.

"Why would these characters bother to transport this unholy mess?" Tony asked.

"Perhaps a once-over will tell us. Come on!"

Frank was already moving, with Tony on his heels. They stealthily crossed the open space to the derelict car.

Close up it looked even worse. All the windows were smashed, and slivers of broken glass littered the interior. The upholstery dangled in shreds and tatters. The back seat was piled with junk—bolts, hubcaps, twisted wire, a rusty jack handle, and various other useless odds and ends.

Tony surveyed the scene with complete disgust. "There isn't anything here to help with the mercury case. I'd say—"

He broke off as slow footsteps approached the gate from the direction of the dock. Hastily the two boys regained their vantage spot in the doorway, where they could survey the scene with no fear of discovery.

They were barely ensconced there when a man

came through the gate. He was hunched way over, his hands cupped together at the waist, suggesting that he carried a heavy burden concealed under his coat. Two more, similarly bent forward, followed him in single file up to the wreck.

Gingerly the first man looked around, lowered a mercury flask to the pavement, and took a funnel from his pocket. He placed it in the opening to the gas tank, heaved his flask into the air, and turned it upside down over the funnel. The mercury ran out, down into the interior of the car.

As soon as he stepped away with the empty flask, the next one took his place, then the third. After they were finished, they walked back through the gate toward the dock, only to be replaced by three more who went through the same motions. The two groups alternated for quite some time.

"Say," Tony marveled, "that heap must have a gigantic gas tank!"

"A gigantic tank, anyway. No car holds that much. They must have put a special tank in to use for this operation. What a gimmick! Who's going to challenge the battered wreck of a defunct car? They could waltz down Main Street in Bayport in total safety!"

The men were still pouring mercury into the tank when a policeman came strolling along, swinging his nightstick, glancing alertly around.

The man heaved his mercury flask into the air

The men at the wreck caught his eye. Curious, he moved in their direction to investigate. At precisely that moment the sounds of a heated dispute broke the stillness. Two sailors lurched out of the shadows.

"All right! All right!" one yelled. "Put 'em up and we'll settle this here and now! No need of a referee to pick the winner!"

"You're on!" screamed the other. "I may be drunk, but I can sure finish you off!"

As the sailors appeared about to pummel one another fiercely, the officer hustled over. "Break it up! You guys have had too much to drink. Better sleep it off!" Taking each by the arm, he pushed them down an alley toward a flophouse for seamen at the opposite end.

"Decoys?" Tony asked Frank in a subdued tone of voice.

"Yes," Frank replied. "Those two were a couple of good-luck charms for the mercury mugs. Gangsters working this kind of a job don't leave much to chance. They must have kept tabs on the timetable of the police patrolling the waterfront. And they were prepared to lure unwelcome representatives of the law away from the center of operations."

"Their plan succeeded brilliantly," Tony commented, pointing to the wreck. No one was to be seen. The men with the flasks had finished their work and had melted away in the darkness. Silence, and shadows rendered sharper by the fitful glare of the street lights, had descended over the area.

"Too bad we didn't have a chance to warn that policeman," Tony remarked. "Still, one man couldn't very well have taken on all of those guys."

"Not only that, but we'd have alerted the ring-leaders. If they knew that we saw the derelict auto, and how it figures in their plans, they would have disappeared by now. And we'd only have netted a few underlings at best."

"True. What's our next step?"

Frank looked at his watch. "Just past midnight. I'm sure they won't do anything with this wreck until the activity starts around here in the early-morning hours, or even later! If they carted it away in the middle of the night, it would alert the harbor police."

"We might have to go after Joe and the others on the ship," Tony said.

"Truc. Tell you what. You wait hcrc and kccp an eye on the car, while I get the police. They can stake out this area and wait for those thieves, in case we have to leave."

Frank left Tony in the doorway and walked around the block until he met a policeman. He explained the situation and the officer went to a call box and phoned his report to Captain Stein.

Fifteen minutes later the captain and a patrol

car full of police arrived at the spot. Frank showed them the wreck and the doorway where he and Tony had hidden out.

Captain Stein praised the boys' detective work. "That was a great job! We'll give those crooks a real reception when they come back for the stuff."

He issued orders to stake out the area. Frank and Tony took their places and everyone settled down to wait for their prey to walk into the trap. Hours ticked by. Frank's eyelids began to droop due to the lack of sleep, and Tony, sitting in the doorway, fell into a short and fitful slumber.

Finally dawn broke. Activity began along the waterfront and the noise jolted the boys into a tense alert. Cars and trucks drove up and down the street. By early morning the tasks of loading and unloading the many ships were in full swing.

Tony spotted the quarry, a wrecker, trundling toward the car. The driver pulled up ahead of it. He and his partner climbed out, went around to the rear, and started fastening ropes to the battered vehicle they had come to fetch.

Then a figure appeared out of nowhere. "Hold it!" Captain Stein ordered. "Police! Stand where you are!"

Instead of standing where they were, the pair took to their heels, bolting in opposite directions. The driver ran directly into the arms of three officers at the corner of a warehouse. They quickly overpowered him and snapped on handcuffs.

His partner was hitting top speed when Tony downed him with a tackle. Frank piled on to make sure of the capture. After being hauled to their feet, the two fugitives stood panting and glowering beside a patrol car.

"So we meet once again!" Frank addressed the pair sarcastically.

They were the hoods from Bayport!

CHAPTER XVIII

Joe Leaves a Clue

CAPTAIN Stein confronted the pair. "What are your names?" he demanded.

The beefy member of the duo nudged his partner to remain silent while he handled the situation. "We're not saying a thing!" he grated with a sullen stare. "We want to see a lawyer. We got our rights, and we'll have your badge for false arrest. You can't push innocent people around!"

"We'll see how innocent you are! Turn around and put your hands on the hood of the car!"

The men were frisked. Papers they had on them gave their names as Clyde Cheever and Russ Bucko. They insisted that they were in the towing business, and that their only interest in the wreck was for scrap.

"Nothing incriminating, Captain?" Frank inquired as the officer shuffled the papers taken from the two.

"Nothing, except the fact that they were trying to make off with a shipment of stolen mercury. That's enough to book them. Then I can have their story about the towing business checked out."

"We know they're lying, Captain," Tony remarked. "They tried to scare Frank and Joe off the mercury case several times. Why would they do that if they're on the up-and-up?"

"You've put it in a nutshell, young man."

Cheever and Bucko were taken away in the patrol car. The last the boys saw of them they were scowling menacingly.

Frank turned to Captain Stein. "Our friends and my brother are on the *Bombay Batarang* and were supposed to meet us here at dawn. We assume they ran into trouble."

"Would you like us to board the ship?"

"Tony and I will try it alone first."

"What'll be our strategy, Frank?" Tony asked.

"Level with the ship's captain and tell him what's up."

"Suppose he's in with the gang?"

"Then we're sunk. But we haven't much choice. Captain Stein, suppose you send a backup squad if you don't hear from us in a couple of hours?"

"Sure thing. I wouldn't let you go if I wasn't convinced that the captain is an honest man. I've met him a few times, and he has a fine reputation.

I think you'll be all right. Someone on his ship is in league with the gang, though, and we'll have to check out the whole crew if you don't come up with something. Good luck!"

Frank and Tony hustled down to the dock, climbed aboard the freighter, and asked to be taken to the captain. He was on the bridge.

Frank recounted the story of the mercury that had been stolen from the cargo.

"This is preposterous!" the captain fumed. "How could so many flasks be removed without anyone on the ship being aware of it?"

"Somebody must have seen the thieves," Frank agreed. "The operation could not have succeeded without assistance from someone on this freighter!"

The captain looked startled. "Do you suspect any member of my crew? Rest assured, I'll find out who he is before we leave Baltimore!"

Tony inquired about Joe, Phil, and Nathoo Keeka.

The captain chuckled. "We have an American boy on board. He is in my cabin, resting."

Frank tensed. "Is there something wrong with him?"

"He suffered a blow on the head that rendered him unconscious yesterday. And he told me that he lost his two companions on the ship. We searched everywhere but did not find them."

Frank and Tony looked at each other apprehensively. "They must have followed a lead and left the ship," Frank said.

"But where did they go?" Tony queried.

Frank heaved a sigh. "That's anybody's guess. When did you look for them, Captain?"

"Yesterday evening."

"Can we see our friend in your cabin now?" Frank asked.

"Certainly." The captain signaled a crewman. "Jawal will take you there."

Was it Joe or Phil? both boys wondered as they followed the Indian down a narrow corridor.

Seconds later they had the answer. "Phil!" cried Tony as he pushed the cabin door open.

"Boy, I'm glad you're here," Phil said. He looked pale and still suffered a severe headache. Quickly he explained the events of the previous day.

"We'd better start searching for Joe and Nathoo right away," Phil suggested. "Matter of fact, I was just on my way to the captain to tell him I was leaving the ship."

"Do you feel up to it?" Frank inquired.

"Oh, sure. But getting rapped on the head with a blunt instrument is something I don't recommend for a rest cure."

"Do you have any leads to work on? Anything you may have noticed while casing the ship before you got conked?"

"One thing. I think the assistant engineer is

one of the gang. Fellow named Luckman Kann. He was pretty put out when we came aboard. Didn't want us to see anything on the ship, least of all the mercury. I suspect he's the one who ambushed me on the bridge!"

The boys passed this information on to the captain, who sent for the assistant engineer. But Luckman Kann was missing!

Frank, Tony, and Phil began a search, starting at the spot where Phil had last seen Joe and Nathoo, and extending over the side down onto the dock.

"The barge has been moved," Phil commented. "It was riding behind the freighter when we went aboard yesterday."

"What's this?" Tony stared at a strip of black leather lying on the dock, pointing toward the place where the barge had been moored. He picked it up and examined the silver buckle at one end. The initials J. H. were engraved on it!

"Joe's belt!" Frank exclaimed exultantly. "He must have put it there so we'd know where he'd gone. All we have to do now is to find out the destination of the barge."

From a stevedore he learned that it had transported bales of jute to a warehouse along the waterfront. The three boys walked away from the docks to avoid being conspicuous, took a parallel street, and cut back down to the dock area. Soon they came to an enormous, dingy building, blackened by soot, and with several windows boarded up.

Tony and Phil staked out the warehouse, while Frank sneaked through some bushes, edged along one wall to a rickety wooden door, and slipped inside. He found himself in a gloomy, cavernous building. The ceiling towered far above his head. Its crossbeams extended from one side of the warehouse to the other.

Boxes and crates were stacked on top of one another. Bales of jute, looking like huge cubes, awaited transfer to the mills. Steel bars, each ending in a heavy bolt, lay in disorderly heaps where they had been dumped.

Frank examined one. It was the type of bolt that had crashed through the window of the Hardys' house!

The boy surveyed the layout of the warehouse, noting that the back door led onto the platform where the barge cargoes came in. The office was at the far side, a mere cubbyhole in the vastness of the interior.

Frank ducked around cartons and crates, lay down on his stomach to snake-crawl past a pile of reinforcement bars, and reached a point where he could see through a dirty window into the dimly lighted office. Figures became discernible. Frank rose on one knee for a better view.

Suddenly his sixth sense warned him that somebody was sneaking up on him. He twisted sharply to one side and bounded to his feet, hands up to ward off an assailant.

Then he dropped his arms. "Joe!" he gasped.

Joe put a finger to his lips and beckoned his brother to retreat with him behind some stacks of cargo. "Don't make any noise," he whispered. "We'll be in a tough spot if those birds come flying out at us!"

Quickly Joe briefed Frank on what had happened on board the *Bombay Batarang*. He and Nathoo had been walking behind Phil when they heard one of the officers mention the Bombay Boomerang on the telephone. It was Luckman Kann! When the assistant engineer hung up, the boys had melted into a doorway, then followed him onto the barge. They had concealed themselves behind bales of jute. The only clue Joe had time to leave was his belt, a signal he hoped Frank would read.

"Good idea," Frank murmured. "Without it we still wouldn't know where you were. But where's Nathoo?"

"They got him!" Joe said grimly and continued his story.

"Kann stayed on the barge till it left early in the morning. We hid during the ride along the waterfront. When the barge stopped, we could see the warehouse, so I got out at the rear while the stevedores were opening the side doors. Nathoo wasn't so lucky. They caught him and marched him into the warehouse."

"How did you get in here?"

"By way of a broken window. I was just wondering how to handle this situation when you showed up!"

"All right, let's join forces and see what's up in the office over there."

A piercing scream rent the silence, bouncing echoes off the walls and ceiling. "They must be beating Nathoo," Joe whispered. "We've got to get him out of there!"

Reaching the window, they looked in. Nathoo was sitting on a chair, tied hand and foot. His face was bruised where he had been struck by the four men who held him captive. Luckman Kann stood to one side, watching with approval. Next to him was the sinister Indian sailor who had tripped Joe into the hold of the *Nanda Kailash*, and who had instigated Nathoo to murder the Hardys.

"You're going to tell us about the Hardys," one man threatened viciously, "if we have to beat you all day!"

Nathoo groaned but remained silent.

"What happened to Cheever and Bucko?" another demanded in violent tones. "They went off after the mercury and now we don't know where they are!"

"I know nothing," Nathoo pleaded. "Nothing at all!"

Frank placed his lips close to Joe's ear. "The police have those goons in custody. I'll tell you about it later."

One of Nathoo's tormentors decided that their third degree would not force any information out of him. "Where are we going to get rid of this bum?" he asked savagely.

"The harbor, of course," a confederate retorted. "A little cement will do the trick."

A confused conversation followed until Frank and Joe caught the following dialogue:

"Is the plane ready?"

"Yes."

"Good. We'll be in the air in plenty of time to complete the job. The Super S will home in right on target!"

The Hardys held their breath in the hope of hearing more about the missing missile. What they actually heard was a ferocious barking on the other side of the warehouse. A powerful mastiff came barreling down on them, fangs bared!

CHAPTER XIX

The Nerve-Gas Plot

THE Hardys plunged headlong behind some bales of jute for protection, but the burly mastiff was nearly on them! With snapping fangs, it gave a tremendous spring over the barrier.

A shot rang out. The dog fell onto the top bale of jute, yelping in pain. Slipping off, it tumbled to the floor and lay still.

"You fool!" a voice rasped. "Why did you shoot? The watchdog would have killed them for us. Now we'll have to do the job ourselves!"

By now Frank and Joe had vanished. Using the bales for a screen, they sneaked along the wall to a pile of reinforcement bars and crouched low.

But one of the gang who had circled around spotted them. He raised his gun and fired. With a loud clang the bullet ricocheted off steel about six inches from Frank's head.

A second shot barely missed Joe. A clatter of

footsteps warned of the gang converging quickly on that part of the warehouse.

"Joe, this way!" Frank said in a hoarse whisper, and raced toward the middle of the building. There he dived headlong behind a stack of cartons. Joe was right on his heels. Panting, they peered around the corner of the pile.

The men were scouting the floor in the vicinity of the reinforcement bars. "We've lost them!" one growled in disgust. "Go over this place with a fine-toothed comb. We don't have to worry as long as they don't get out alive!"

The pursuers were approaching the stack of cartons. Frank and Joe dashed toward another pile of jute. Bullets cut into the floor as the gang caught sight of them and opened up with a hail of lead.

Then the shooting stopped. "We've got 'em! They're penned in! Hold your fire!" came a voice.

Wildly Frank and Joe looked around. They were boxed into a corner of the warehouse. Suddenly Frank seized Joe by the arm and pointed to a ladder. It led up the wall to a platform on the crossbeams overhead.

"You go first," he hissed. "Don't move until I create a diversion to cover the retreat!"

He picked up a rusty pail standing in the corner. Balancing it in his hand, he lobbed it beyond the cargo, where it careened noisily along the floor. Whirling around, the gang sent a fusillade after it. Slugs tore into the pail, causing it to spin and bounce crazily.

Joe scrambled up the ladder to the platform before the men below realized they had been tricked. Frank made it by inches as bullets splintered under his foot.

Rough hands gripped the ladder. Heavy feet hit the rungs. The boys were about to have company.

No retreat was left except across the platform. "Another ladder!" Frank panted as they reached the opposite end. They slid down to the racket of feet pounding after them. They found themselves near the front door and ran outside.

To their enormous relief, they were greeted by a group of policemen! Tony and Phil had given the alarm when they heard the first shot in the warehouse!

The gang came rushing out the door into the arms of the officers.

Led by Frank and Joe, the policemen entered the warehouse office and released Nathoo who, despite his bruises, was not seriously injured. He promised to testify against the criminals, all of whom proved to be ex-convicts wanted for armed robbery in seaports along the East Coast.

Mission accomplished, Phil and Tony returned home. Frank and Joe, after phoning their father, made arrangements to meet him in Washington for a top-priority meeting with Admiral Rodgers.

During the ride to the Pentagon, Fenton Hardy told the boys some dramatic news.

"Chief Collig got a report on the thumbprint you left with him. Teddy Blaze has a record. Started as a boy delinquent, graduated to the rank of thief, and became a disk jockey in prison."

Frank let out a low whistle. "I thought so!"

"That's not all. Collig thinks Blaze may be the ringleader of a gang of thieves operating in the East. He also suspects that this ring may have been infiltrated by agents of a foreign power."

Upon arriving at the Pentagon, the Hardys went directly to Admiral Rodgers' office, who listened soberly to the detective's summation of the case. Frank and Joe added their own comments.

"You've gathered so much information," the admiral said, "that there's no point in holding back on the rest of what we know. I told you that the tape from Commander Wenn's office contained classified data. Well, here's the story:

"One of the voices on the tape mentioned Colorado. The government has nerve gas stored there underground, in natural caves. There's been some talk about this—residents complaining about the danger if an earthquake tremor should split the ground and the stuff got out into the air. One farmer charges that his cattle have already been affected by leakage."

Mr. Hardy frowned. "Is that true?"

"No. All of these accusations are unfounded.

The gas is in containers that can't be cracked by an earthquake and are leakproof. The real peril is that someone might use artificial means to release it. I mean, explosives!"

Frank and Joe looked at their father, who stared at the admiral. None of them had realized the deadly nature of the threat to the nation.

"I see you're startled," Rodgers went on. "So were we when we listened to the tape the first time. Another angle. Army intelligence found a wooden shack in the woods near where the nerve gas is stored. Brand new, and clearly put up in a hurry after the last patrol had been through the area. Inside was a large electrical heating unit."

"A heating unit?" Frank repeated. "For what?"

"The thing puzzled us, too. If it had been a cache of dynamite, the explanation would be simple. Enemy agents intended to touch off an explosion that would break the crust of the earth, crack the gas containers, and turn the lethal vapor loose. An electrical heating unit didn't seem to make much sense."

"Is it still there?" Joe inquired.

"Yes, but inoperable. We took no chances. A couple of key parts were removed in utmost secrecy. Of course we didn't want to scare the agents off."

"Let's see," Mr. Hardy said thoughtfully. "We've got a missile missing, a store of highly dangerous nerve gas, an electrical heating unit—"

"There's the connection, Dad!" Frank burst out. "The Super S is programmed for heat. Whoever has the missile must have set up that heating unit in Colorado! They want to send the Super S crashing into it with enough force to smash both the cave ceilings and the nerve-gas containers!"

The admiral nodded. "That's what we figured."

"And there's the explanation of the Bombay Boomerang!" Joe put in, barely able to control his excitement. "We've been assuming that Bombay is one word because we've only heard it spoken. We never saw it written down."

"I get you," Frank said. "It might be two words: *Bomb bay*. The Super S is an air-to-ground missile. So bomb bay would refer to the fact that it's launched from an airplane! And the crooks said the plane was ready!"

Mr. Hardy spoke up. "Boomerang also makes sense. The whole operation has been planned to make the nerve gas boomerang on the United States. It's a great code word!"

"Your theory sounds perfectly plausible," Admiral Rodgers said gravely. "Military precautions must be taken without delay. I'll start the ball rolling by informing the Secretary of Defense and the Joint Chiefs of Staff. Are you going back to Bayport now?"

Mr. Hardy nodded. "I think our mission here is accomplished."

The admiral pressed a buzzer and an aide came in. "Order a car for these gentlemen, please!" Rodgers said, and the aide disappeared.

"Mr. Hardy, I'm grateful to you and your sons," the admiral said to the detective. "You've done a fine job. Your car will be here in about ten minutes. Meanwhile, I'd better get to work."

He escorted the Hardys to the elevator and shook hands all around. Seconds later the Hardys emerged on the ground floor and made their way to a spot outside where official cars pulled in to pick up passengers.

A car driven by a chauffeur eased up to the curb. A second man in uniform got out and opened the back door with a deferential bow to the Hardys. "Your limousine, gentlemen."

Mr. Hardy laughed. "The U. S. Navy is a lot speedier than Admiral Rodgers imagines!"

"Yes, sir," the man replied smoothly. "We do our best to please. If you will get in, we'll have you at the airport in a jiffy."

As the Hardys climbed in, the uniformed man slammed the door and rejoined the chauffeur in the front. The car took off with a jolt that threw the passengers against the back seat. They swished down the drive, through the Pentagon grounds, and out into the street.

"He came fast and he's going even faster," Mr. Hardy remarked, rubbing his elbow where it had hit the armrest.

"We'd better tell him to take it a little easier," Frank proposed. "We're not in that much of a hurry."

"Besides, we're liable to pile into somebody," Joe added as the car snaked swiftly through the maze of traffic.

"Say!" Mr. Hardy spoke up in alarm. "This guy isn't going to the airport. He must be a numbskull as well as a cowboy. We ought to buy him a map of Washington!"

Frank rapped sharply on the glass partition that separated the front and the rear of the limousine. The man next to the driver turned around and gave an evil grin.

"These characters aren't working for the Navy!" Mr. Hardy exploded. "They're phonies! We're being kidnapped!"

CHAPTER XX

Secret in the Air

THE man leering at them slid open the glass panel on his side of the car. A long, narrow cylinder appeared in his hand, pointing straight into the back seat.

"A pencil gun," Joe muttered. "Just what the well-dressed thug is wearing this year."

Frank spoke with barbed sarcasm. "Excuse me, but you seem to be headed in the wrong direction."

"Have fun while you can, wise guy!" the man snapped. "You don't have an awful lot of time left!"

"Mind telling us where we're going?" Mr. Hardy inquired.

"You're the detective. Take a guess!" The driver sniggered at his partner's humor. The two were enjoying themselves.

The limousine swung deeper into Virginia, and

turned off into a lonely wooded section where tall trees shaded thick undergrowth. Residential districts had been left far behind. Only hunters were likely to be seen in this part of the state. And even they would not be coming through until months later when the hunting season began.

"I'll tell you a secret," the driver said. "We're on our way to a funeral. Your funeral. We've got a hole in the ground already dug for you."

"I would like to register a protest." Joe was talking tongue-in-cheek. "I'm allergic to funerals, especially my own."

"Actually," the second man commented, "I'm glad it worked out this way. There wasn't any sense in giving you guys all those warnings to get off the mercury case. Cheever and Bucko dreamed that up. They always were a couple of dimwits. We'll see to it that our method is more effective."

Frank decided to trick the two thugs into revealing more information. "Well, one good threat deserves another. You might as well forget about operation Bomb Bay Boomerang. You'll never get away with it now."

"That's what you think. It'll work out all right. And there'll be a hot time in the old USA when it hits. That nerve gas will knock out enough people to start riots from coast to coast. The government will be overthrown."

Fenton Hardy knitted his brows. "The last piece of the jigsaw puzzle has just fallen into place. Mercury fulminate is an explosive used for such things as cartridge detonators. You plan to put the liquid metal and the missing missile together!"

"Smart guy. You guessed it. We've developed a super warhead made of mercury fulminate. Get the picture? The bomb sets up shock waves so devastating they can crack the crust of the earth for miles and miles!"

"How?"

"You'll keep our secret—you won't be alive to tell it. The missile will home in on a heating unit we've set up in Colorado right under the nose of the military. We'll get the underground defenses one after the other. The gas will be all over the state in a matter of minutes, with a terrific toll!"

The driver glanced at his watch and snapped on the radio. "Time to listen to a little music," he said.

Teddy Blaze's program came on. Stomping rhythms blared for a couple of minutes before the disk jockey stopped the recordings and went into his patter.

"Endsville for now, chums. Midnight tonight our program will leave Bayport. Good-by, Balto. Deadline for the big shakeup. Are you with me out there? Let's go, one and all!"

The driver clicked the radio off.

"So," Frank reasoned aloud, "the troops are being called in from Baltimore. Your plane will leave tonight with the Super S aboard from Bayport, bound for Colorado!"

The two gangsters in the front seat were visibly astonished by the accuracy of the deduction.

"You know about Blaze, do you?" snarled the driver. "Cracked his code? Never mind. When you are out of the way, no one will be any wiser."

"Tell me," Joe said amiably, "where did you hide the Super S?"

"In Teddy's garage in Bayport. Good place, eh? He was building an addition, so the truck which delivered the missile also carried some roofing sheets and cement. All in order." The man chuckled.

His partner, however, objected to his frankness. He nudged him. "Get to the graveyard fast. I want to plant these characters."

The car picked up speed along a rough dirt road. Branches scraped the sides as it lurched over boulders and down into potholes, jouncing those inside up and down until they reached for the nearest support.

Taking advantage of the jolting ride, Joe leaned down toward the floor. The man with the pencil gun pushed his hand through the partition. "Sit up," he ordered, "or I'll see to it that you stay down permanently!"

Joe came up with a karate kick that slammed the thug against the dashboard. Reacting instantaneously, Mr. Hardy reached through the partition, grabbed the driver by the arm, twisting it until he yelled with pain.

The car, out of control, careened wildly off the road. Bouncing across a gully, it zoomed into a clearing, hit a massive tree with a swipe that caused the vehicle to turn over, and came to rest back on its wheels.

Frank and Joe were thrown clear as the impact jarred a back door open. Mr. Hardy and the two abductors were still inside, but out cold.

Frank sat up. "Joe—Joe, are you all right?"

Joe answered with a grunt. "I hope so. Where's Dad?"

"Still in the car."

While the boys were picking themselves up, a patrol car stopped by the side of the road. Several policemen led by Captain Stein piled out and rushed across to the limousine.

"Just in time!" Frank called out in relief.

"We've been tailing you ever since you left the Pentagon," the captain explained. "Your real driver saw you go off with these phonies. He checked with the admiral, then told us you were being kidnapped."

"He was right," Frank said dryly.

The three occupants of the limousine were lifted out onto the grass. "They'll be okay," one of the officers declared. "Temporarily separated from their senses. Nothing worse. In fact, they're coming around now."

Frank and Joe were kneeling anxiously at their father's side. Mr. Hardy soon revived and gave an account of the abduction at the Pentagon, and said he would prefer charges against the hoodlums.

The two prisoners, glaring in anger, were marched to the squad car as soon as they could walk. Two more police cars arrived with reinforcements.

"National security is involved," Joe told the captain. "We must get back to Bayport as fast as we can."

"No problem. Get into the first car, and we'll take you to the airport in no time."

Minutes later, the car reached the highway, and with siren screaming for traffic to get out of the way, sped to the Washington airport. After thanking Captain Stein for his help, the Hardys quickly joined Jack Wayne on their private plane for the flight home.

"What's our next step?" Joe asked when they were airborne.

"The gang's plane won't leave until midnight," Mr. Hardly replied. "We might as well go home and be back by eleven. That should give us enough time to stop the take-off."

"Shall we alert the airport police?" Frank asked.

"No. Admiral Rodgers wants as few people as possible to know about the whole thing. We'll handle this ourselves. But I'll call him as soon as we land about having FBI men on hand."

The plane touched down in Bayport and the Hardys took a taxi home. Mrs. Hardy gave them an affectionate welcome. Aunt Gertrude opined crisply that they would have done better if they had stayed in Bayport.

"If this is where the action is, what was the point of going to Baltimore?"

Joe grinned. "Well, Aunty, we couldn't have known where the action is if we hadn't dug up clues in Baltimore."

"And we did have a rather exciting time when we were there," Frank added.

"In any case," Joe said, "you'll be glad to hear that we expect to conclude this case tonight."

"I hope so!" Miss Hardy said. "It's about time that you stayed home for a while!"

Frank called his friends and asked them to come over. Soon they arrived in Biff's car, Chet with an armful of boomerangs.

"Since we might have some spare time on our hands," he announced, "I brought something to occupy us."

Before the Hardy boys could answer, their father came dashing out the door. "Admiral Rodgers just called. He's picked up some information that the midnight flight has been changed. The plane will take off earlier!"

Frank and Joe were aghast. "We've got to leave right away!" Frank exclaimed.

"Right. Hurry up!"

"What's going on?" Biff asked.

"We'll tell you later," Frank said. "Just follow us!" He jumped behind the wheel of their convertible. Mr. Hardy and Joe slid in beside him. When they reached the airport they sped directly out to the runway.

A private, single-engine jet was gathering speed for take-off. Blazoned on its nose was a large crimson boomerang!

"That's the plane!" Joe yelled. "What can we do to stop it?"

"Use our boomerangs!" Chet quickly threw a couple to each of his friends.

As the jet roared past a few feet from where they were standing, the boys hurled a barrage of weapons at it. Two struck the air intake, and were sucked in, causing the engine to quit. The plane slowed to a halt.

Teddy Blaze, glowering furiously, shook his fists at the boys through the window.

Joe chuckled. "I guess he knows by now that although we're not his most enthusiastic music fans, we do have a certain interest in his career!"

FBI agents swarmed aboard the plane. Overpowering the thugs who made a brief resistance, they cleared the intake. An FBI pilot turned the craft around and taxied back to the hangar, where Blaze and his confederates were removed in handcuffs for the trip to jail.

The pilot flipped a switch, and while the Hardys and their friends, who had followed the plane in their cars, looked on, the bomb-bay door swung down.

A glistening cigar-shaped missile came into view, perched in its rack, complete with sinister warhead, programming mechanism, and spreading tail fins.

The Super S!

The Hardys' friends stared in utter amazement. While Frank and Joe filled them in on the importance of their caper, Mr. Hardy left to phone the Pentagon. When he returned, he addressed the group of boys with him.

"Admiral Rodgers is very relieved that the conspirators were caught before they could launch their attack. He says the final report by his staff shows that Teddy Blaze is indeed the gang leader who mixed crime instructions with his music patter over the radio."

Chet whistled. "And before Frank and Joe suspected him, we thought he was just a kooky talker!"

Mr. Hardy nodded and went on. "The Blaze gang has been stealing defense secrets and military hardware for a foreign power. They were on such an assignment when they ransacked Commander Wenn's office for the Super S data."

"And we got involved when I dialed the wrong number and got the Pentagon!" Joe said.

"Exactly. The same foreign power paid for the theft of the mercury, and even sent an airman to pilot the plane to Colorado. They set up the heating unit for the missile to home in on."

"Which foreign power?" Frank asked.

"The admiral is not at liberty to say," his father replied. "One more thing. We're receiving a commendation from the Defense Department for services to the nation."

He was about to turn back to the car when a sudden thought struck him. "You know," he said with a smile, "one of us did more than the rest to ground that plane. I think he deserves a special vote of thanks."

Chet grinned and held up a hand. "Say no more, sir. I get the message. The Bomb Bay Boomerang was knocked out by a Chet Morton Special!"

The laughter and banter that followed put everyone in a happy, relaxed mood. But it was not to last long, because another mystery—*Danger on Vampire Trail*—soon was destined to test the sleuthing ability of the Hardy boys.

Order Form
New revised editions of
THE BOBBSEY TWINS®

In *hardcover* at your local bookseller OR
simply mail in this handy order coupon and start your collection today!

Mail order form to: PUTNAM PUBLISHING GROUP/Mail Order Department
390 Murray Hill Parkway, East Rutherford, NJ 07073

ORDERED BY

Name _____

Address _____

City & State _____ Zip Code _____

Please send me the following Bobbsey Twins titles I've checked below.
All Books Priced @ $4.95

AVOID DELAYS Please Print Order Form Clearly

☐ 1. Of Lakeport   448-09071-6   ☐ 8. Big Adventure at Home   448-09134-8
☐ 2. Adventure in the Country   448-09072-4   ☐ 10. On Blueberry Island   448-40110-X
☐ 3. Secret at the Seashore   448-09073-2   ☐ 11. Mystery on the
☐ 4. Mystery at School   448-09074-0   Deep Blue Sea   448-40113-4
☐ 5. At Snow Lodge   448-09098-8   ☐ 12. Adventure in
☐ 6. On a Houseboat   448-09099-6   Washington   448-40111-8
☐ 7. Mystery at Meadowbrook   448-09100-3   ☐ 13. Visit to the Great West 448-40112-6

Own the original exciting
BOBBSEY TWINS® ADVENTURE STORIES
still available:

☐ 13. Visit to the Great West   448-08013-3
☐ 14. And the Cedar Camp Mystery   448-08014-1

ALL ORDERS MUST BE PREPAID   Postage and Handling Charges as follows

_____ Payment Enclosed $2.00 for one book

_____ Visa $ .50 for each additional book thereafter

_____ Mastercard-Interbank #   *(Maximum charge of $4.95)*

Card # _____   Merchandise total   _____

                                           Shipping and Handling _____
Expiration Date _____
                                           Applicable Sales Tax   _____

Signature _____   Total Amount
(Minimum Credit Card order of $10.00)   *(U.S. currency only)*   [   ]

The Bobbsey Twins series is a trademark of Simon & Schuster, Inc.,
and is registered in the United States Patent and Trademark Office.

Please allow 4 to 6 weeks for delivery.

DETACH ALONG DOTTED LINE AND MAIL IN ENVELOPE WITH PAYMENT

Order Form

Own the original 58 action-packed

HARDY BOYS MYSTERY STORIES®

In *hardcover* at your local bookseller OR
simply mail in this handy order coupon and start your collection today!

Mail order form to   PUTNAM PUBLISHING GROUP/Mail Order Department
390 Murray Hill Parkway, East Rutherford, NJ 07073

ORDERED BY
Name _____

Address _____

City & State _____   Zip Code _____

Please send me the following Hardy Boys titles I've checked below
All Books Priced @ $4.95.

AVOID DELAYS   Please Print Order Form Clearly

☐ 1. Tower Treasure	448-08901-7	
☐ 2. House on the Cliff	448-08902-5	
☐ 3. Secret of the Old Mill	448-08903-3	
☐ 4. Missing Chums	448-08904-1	
☐ 5. Hunting for Hidden Gold	448-08905-X	
☐ 6. Shore Road Mystery	448-08906-8	
☐ 7. Secret of the Caves	448-08907-6	
☐ 8. Mystery of Cabin Island	448-08908-4	
☐ 9. Great Airport Mystery	448-08909-2	
☐ 10. What Happened at Midnight	448-08910-6	
☐ 11. While the Clock Ticked	448-08911-4	
☐ 12. Footprints Under the Window	448-08912-2	
☐ 13. Mark on the Door	448-08913-0	
☐ 14. Hidden Harbor Mystery	448-08914-9	
☐ 15. Sinister Sign Post	448-08915-7	
☐ 16. A Figure in Hiding	448-08916-5	
☐ 17. Secret Warning	448-08917-3	
☐ 18. Twisted Claw	448-08918-1	
☐ 19. Disappearing Floor	448-08919-X	
☐ 20. Mystery of the Flying Express	448-08920-3	
☐ 21. The Clue of the Broken Blade	448-08921-1	
☐ 22. The Flickering Torch Mystery	448-08922-X	
☐ 23. Melted Coins	448-08923-8	
☐ 24. Short-Wave Mystery	448-08924-6	
☐ 25. Secret Panel	448-08925-4	
☐ 26. The Phantom Freighter	448-08926-2	
☐ 27. Secret of Skull Mountain	448-08927-0	
☐ 28. The Sign of the Crooked Arrow	448-08928-9	
☐ 29. The Secret of the Lost Tunnel	448-08929-7	
☐ 30. Wailing Siren Mystery	448-08930-0	
☐ 31. Secret of Wildcat Swamp	448-08931-9	
☐ 32. Crisscross Shadow	448-08932-7	
☐ 33. The Yellow Feather Mystery	448-08933-5	
☐ 34. The Hooded Hawk Mystery	448-08934-3	
☐ 35. The Clue in the Embers	448-08935-1	
☐ 36. The Secret of Pirates' Hill	448-08936-X	
☐ 37. Ghost at Skeleton Rock	448-08937-8	
☐ 38. Mystery at Devil's Paw	448-08938-6	
☐ 39. Mystery of the Chinese Junk	448-08939-4	
☐ 40. Mystery of the Desert Giant	448-08940-8	
☐ 41. Clue of the Screeching Owl	448-08941-6	
☐ 42. Viking Symbol Mystery	448-08942-4	
☐ 43. Mystery of the Aztec Warrior	448-08943-2	
☐ 44. The Haunted Fort	448-08944-0	
☐ 45. Mystery of the Spiral Bridge	448-08945-9	
☐ 46. Secret Agent on Flight 101	448-08946-7	
☐ 47. Mystery of the Whale Tattoo	448-08947-5	
☐ 48. The Arctic Patrol Mystery	448-08948-3	
☐ 49. The Bombay Boomerang	448-08949-1	
☐ 50. Danger on Vampire Trail	448-08950-5	
☐ 51. The Masked Monkey	448-08951-3	
☐ 52. The Shattered Helmet	448-08952-1	
☐ 53. The Clue of the Hissing Serpent	448-08953-X	
☐ 54. The Mysterious Caravan	448-08954-8	
☐ 55. The Witchmaster's Key	448-08955-6	
☐ 56. The Jungle Pyramid	448-08956-4	
☐ 57. The Firebird Rocket	448-08957-2	
☐ 58. The Sting of The Scorpion	448-08958-0	

Also Available The Hardy Boys Detective Handbook 448-01990-6

ALL ORDERS MUST BE PREPAID

_____ Payment Enclosed

_____ Visa

_____ Mastercard-Interbank #

Card # _____

Expiration Date_____

Signature_____
(Minimum Credit Card order of $10.00)

Postage and Handling Charges as follows

$2.00 for one book

$ .50 for each additional book thereafter

(Maximum charge of $4.95)

Merchandise total	_____
Shipping and Handling	_____
Applicable Sales Tax	_____
Total Amount *(U.S. currency only)*	☐

Nancy Drew® and The Hardy Boys® are trademarks of Simon & Schuster, Inc.,
and are registered in the United States Patent and Trademark Office.

Please allow 4 to 6 weeks for delivery

DETACH ALONG DOTTED LINE AND MAIL IN ENVELOPE WITH PAYMENT

Order Form

Own the original 56 thrilling
NANCY DREW MYSTERY STORIES®

In *hardcover* at your local bookseller OR
simply mail in this handy order coupon and start your collection today!

Mail order form to   PUTNAM PUBLISHING GROUP/Mail Order Department
390 Murray Hill Parkway, East Rutherford, NJ 07073

ORDERED BY
Name _____

Address _____

City & State _____ Zip Code _____

Please send me the following Nancy Drew titles I've checked below
All Books Priced @ $4.95.

AVOID DELAYS   Please Print Order Form Clearly

☐	1	Secret of the Old Clock	448-09501-7	☐ 29	Mystery at the Ski Jump	448-09529-7
☐	2	Hidden Staircase	448-09502-5	☐ 30	Clue of the Velvet Mask	448-09530-0
☐	3	Bungalow Mystery	448-09503-3	☐ 31	Ringmaster's Secret	448-09531-9
☐	4	Mystery at Lilac Inn	448-09504-1	☐ 32	Scarlet Slipper Mystery	448-09532-7
☐	5	Secret of Shadow Ranch	448-09505-X	☐ 33	Witch Tree Symbol	448-09533-5
☐	6	Secret of Red Gate Farm	448-09506-8	☐ 34	Hidden Window Mystery	448-09534-3
☐	7	Clue in the Diary	448-09507-6	☐ 35	Haunted Showboat	448-09535-1
☐	8	Nancy's Mysterious Letter	448-09508-4	☐ 36	Secret of the Golden Pavilion	448-09536-X
☐	9	The Sign of the Twisted Candles	448-09509-2	☐ 37	Clue in the Old Stagecoach	448-09537-8
☐	10	Password to Larkspur Lane	448-09510-6	☐ 38	Mystery of the Fire Dragon	448-09538-6
☐	11	Clue of the Broken Locket	448-09511-4	☐ 39	Clue of the Dancing Puppet	448-09539-4
☐	12	The Message in the Hollow Oak	448-09512-2	☐ 40	Moonstone Castle Mystery	448-09540-8
☐	13	Mystery of the Ivory Charm	448-09513-0	☐ 41	Clue of the Whistling Bagpipes	448-09541-6
☐	14	The Whispering Statue	448-09514-9	☐ 42	Phantom of Pine Hill	448-09542-4
☐	15	Haunted Bridge	448-09515-7	☐ 43	Mystery of the 99 Steps	448-09543-2
☐	16	Clue of the Tapping Heels	448-09516-5	☐ 44	Clue in the Crossword Cipher	448-09544-0
☐	17	Mystery of the Brass-Bound Trunk	448-09517-3	☐ 45	Spider Sapphire Mystery	448-09545-9
☐	18	Mystery at Moss-Covered Mansion	448-09518-1	☐ 46	The Invisible Intruder	448-09546-7
☐	19	Quest of the Missing Map	448-09519-X	☐ 47	The Mysterious Mannequin	448-09547-5
☐	20	Clue in the Jewel Box	448-09520-3	☐ 48	The Crooked Banister	448-09548-3
☐	21	The Secret in the Old Attic	448-09521-1	☐ 49	The Secret of Mirror Bay	448-09549-1
☐	22	Clue in the Crumbling Wall	448-09522-X	☐ 50	The Double Jinx Mystery	448-09550-5
☐	23	Mystery of the Tolling Bell	448-09523-8	☐ 51	Mystery of the Glowing Eye	448-09551-3
☐	24	Clue in the Old Album	448-09524-6	☐ 52	The Secret of the Forgotten City	448-09552-1
☐	25	Ghost of Blackwood Hall	448-09525-4	☐ 53	The Sky Phantom	448-09553-X
☐	26	Clue of the Leaning Chimney	448-09526-2	☐ 54	The Strange Message in the Parchment	448-09554-8
☐	27	Secret of the Wooden Lady	448-09527-0	☐ 55	Mystery of Crocodile Island	448-09555-6
☐	28	The Clue of the Black Keys	448-09528-9	☐ 56	The Thirteenth Pearl	448-09556-4

ALL ORDERS MUST BE PREPAID

_____ Payment Enclosed

_____ Visa

_____ Mastercard-Interbank #

Card # _____

Expiration Date_____

Signature_____
(Minimum Credit Card order of $10.00)

Postage and Handling Charges as follows

$2.00 for one book

$ .50 for each additional book thereafter

(Maximum charge of $4.95)

Merchandise total   _____

Shipping and Handling   _____

Applicable Sales Tax   _____

Total Amount   [_____]
(U.S. currency only)

Nancy Drew* and The Hardy Boys* are trademarks of Simon & Schuster, Inc
and are registered in the United States Patent and Trademark Office

Please allow 4 to 6 weeks for delivery

DETACH ALONG DOTTED LINE AND MAIL IN ENVELOPE WITH PAYMENT